SLAVE BOY IN JUDEA

by Josephine Sanger Lau

Cover design by Elle Staples

Cover illustration by Kessler Garrity

This unabridged version has updated grammar and spelling.

First published in 1953

Table of Contents

CHAPTER 1: THE SLAVE MARKET

Madoc was very tired. He stumbled as he climbed the wide stone steps, and his chains clanked noisily. Though he did not lift his head, he knew that he had come to his journey's end. The stone steps led to the Roman slave market at Cremona.

Reaching the doorway, he looked about. Men dressed in rich mantles of many colors were standing together in little groups talking. Against the wall to his left was a wooden platform with three steps leading up to it. On the floor in front of the platform huddled a group of slaves. They were captives, like himself, waiting to be sold.

Madoc did not lift his eyes to the man on the platform. His shouted words beat against Madoc's ears like hammer blows.

"Move on! Move on!" barked the familiar voice of the slave trader behind him.

Madoc shuffled forward. He, with others from his homeland of Gaul, had been moving on for many weary miles in response to that command. Now he took his place and waited in line. After a time the iron bands were removed from his wrists, and his chains fell with a final clank to the tiled floor.

For a moment his whole body felt light and free. A tiny

flame of hope leaped into his blue eyes. They darted to the high barred windows and to the guarded doorway through which he had come. Then the flame died.

A quick shove sent him stumbling toward the group of slaves in front of the platform. Suddenly in the blur of lifted faces, he caught the gleam of white teeth. A dark-skinned African was sitting cross-legged near the foot of the steps. He was smiling directly at Madoc. With a sigh of great weariness, the boy dropped down beside him.

The big African whispered, his lips scarcely moving, "You look pretty tired, lad. Lean back against Hannibal and rest."

Madoc felt a bare brown arm reach out to cushion his sagging back. He tried to sit up straight, then suddenly his whole body collapsed against the supporting arm. Tears burned behind his eyes. He pinched the lids together until they hurt. The sons of Gallic warriors did not weep.

Hannibal had spoken in the language of the hated Romans that Madoc too had been forced to learn. It had a gentler tone on the lips of the dark-skinned slave. Now Madoc listened to the noisy talk of the Roman buyers and, close above his head, the piercing voice of the auctioneer.

After a time he opened his eyes and looked up. The man was holding his hand above the head of a tall, fair-haired girl. She stood gazing straight before her, over the heads of the crowd. Madoc could see that her hands were clenched so tightly that the knuckles showed white.

"See," shouted the auctioneer, "she is beautiful!" He caught her bare arm and lifted it roughly. "Notice, too, she is strong and healthy and young enough to learn."

Madoc closed his eyes again. This time it was even harder to keep back the tears, for the girl reminded him of his mother. The thought of her made him remember his plan, and for a moment his shoulders lifted.

When Madoc leaned back again, two red spots burned on his pale cheeks. He glanced from corner to corner of the big stone pavilion. Suddenly he caught the steady, threatening gaze of the slave trader who had brought him here. The man was watching him as if he could read his thoughts.

Madoc closed his eyes. He pretended to sleep as the bidding went on. Six hundred, eight hundred, a thousand denarii for the girl with the yellow hair!

When it was over, Madoc looked up. The elderly purchaser wore a white robe with a cloak of fine blue wool flung over one shoulder. His face wrinkled into a grin of satisfaction as the girl stumbled down the steps. But her eyes, as she caught Madoc's steady gaze, were dull and hopeless.

Now the Gallic lad turned to look at the other captives awaiting their turn on the auction block. The two young men with shaven chins and long mustaches were, he knew, from the German tribes that lived beyond the Rhine River. He noticed a dark-skinned woman with a high cone of hair extending back from her head. Near her were others with straight black hair, wearing curious bracelets and beads about their necks. The rest were all of his own race—tall, blue-eyed, and fair.

From time to time, one of the group was kicked or prodded into standing up, to be looked over more closely by a Roman buyer.

Madoc's attention was caught by a man who stood close to the platform, yet apart from the other buyers. He was dressed in the coarse brown tunic of a farmer. He looked out of place among the richly clad men of the town.

The man lifted a thick brown hand to rub his chin. Then, as Madoc watched, he pulled a roll of papyrus from the folds of his belt. His lips moved and his head nodded as he read its message.

Suddenly he stared directly at the watching boy. Madoc glanced away quickly, but he knew the man continued to stare.

"Roman farmer watching you, lad," muttered the African. "Don't like Roman farmers."

Madoc's heart skipped a beat. He turned his head a little and leaned more closely against the strong arm at his back. "I hate all Romans!" he whispered.

The brown-clad man was coming closer. His hand was still on his chin, his eyes thoughtful.

Madoc drew back his legs. At a gruff command, he stood up. He did not cringe as the farmer lifted the mat of yellow hair that lay against his neck, then prodded his ribs and jerked his jaw down to examine his teeth.

"Your name?" he asked.

"Madoc."

"Age thirteen, perhaps?"

"Yes."

The farmer frowned. Madoc rubbed his pinched chin and waited. When the man walked away, he sat down again.

After a time a slave dealer prodded the African. With the ease of a jungle tiger, Hannibal's long legs swung him quickly to his feet. Madoc watched as the huge African climbed the three steps to the auction block.

"This man," shouted the auctioneer, "already bears the brand of a slave." He jerked his dark head sidewise. "See, he has the mark of the awl through his ear."

Hannibal looked down and grinned cheerfully at Madoc. The auctioneer studied a roll of papyrus that an assistant held up before him. Then he went on: "This slave belonged to Marius, a baker, who has been imprisoned for debt. Before that, he served a farmer. He has learned to till the soil and care for the horses and cattle and sheep, and he has been trained in the making of bread and honey cakes. What am I offered for this able and powerful servant?"

Madoc listened as the price went up and up. The farmer, he noticed, was bidding for the first time. After each bid, he offered just a little more.

Suddenly it was all over. Hannibal, with a worried frown on

his good-natured face, walked down the steps and went to stand behind the man in the brown tunic.

Madoc's heart thumped against the back of his throat as he saw a guard walking toward him. Without waiting to be kicked, he got to his feet and climbed to the platform. The auctioneer's assistant took from him his cloak and tunic, then pushed him forward, dressed only in a loincloth.

"This lad," shouted the auctioneer, "comes from Gaul, the land beyond the Alps, where men grow tall and strong."

He lifted Madoc's arm and bent it at the elbow. "Already the boy's muscles are firm."

"I see very little muscle of any kind," complained a buyer. "Rather, the lad appears to have been starved and driven, and his bones are slender. He is not built for heavy work."

A man with a high-pitched voice agreed. "I marvel that one so young and tender should be offered for sale. I would as soon think of buying an unweaned colt."

The auctioneer tried to outshout the wave of laughter that passed over the crowd. "But see, his eyes are clear, his face intelligent! He could easily be trained for work in the library of a nobleman. And, in the meantime, he is old enough to serve wherever an extra pair of hands is needed. How much am I offered for this handsome, blue-eyed lad?"

Madoc remembered the girl from his homeland. Like her, he stared boldly straight ahead. His hands, too, were clenched at his sides, and the red spots of his cheeks burned hotly.

He noticed that the bids were coming slowly. Only one man was answering without hesitating after each small rise in price. Without lowering his eyes, Madoc knew it was the farmer.

The man with the high-pitched voice whined, "I have children in plenty. Why buy another?"

More laughter and the red in Madoc's cheeks spread to his neck and forehead. The farmer, however, did not laugh. His bid remained the highest.

"Sold!" shouted the auctioneer after a pause. "Sold, to Gratus, the overseer for Cornelius the centurion."

Madoc was pushed from the platform, his tunic and cloak tossed after him. He covered his body and, with lowered eyes, took his place beside Hannibal. The price had been small, and Gratus' face wore a satisfied smile.

"Come," he said to Madoc and Hannibal, "follow me."

Madoc was cheered a little to know that the huge African was beside him as he walked out of the slave market and down the stone steps.

The red spots still burned in Madoc's cheeks, and his heart was beating thickly. The thing he was about to do—had he not planned it with every step that took him farther from his homeland? It could not—must not fail!

Madoc was hungry and tired. His feet were swollen and bleeding where his sandals had worn through on the rough stone of the Roman roads. But his thoughts were not on his empty stomach and smarting feet. The farmer had reached the corner. He was turning to the left. Madoc dropped back a pace as if to follow without crowding on the narrow walk. His body grew tense as he darted a swift glance to right and left, then a quick look behind. The way was clear.

"Now—now!"

The word formed on his lips without a sound. A sharp turn to the right and he sped away, sure-footed as a forest deer.

CHAPTER 2: A WORN-OUT SANDAL

There was a moment of silence behind, then a startled cry from Hannibal.

"After him!" shouted the farmer. The voice, hoarse with anger, lent wings to Madoc's flying feet.

Now came the African, pad-pad-padding in tremendous strides, his long legs eating up the distance between them.

Madoc's hunted eyes searched wildly for a way of escape. A sharp turn into a side street and he gained a stride on the heavier Hannibal.

An opening! He cried silently. A place to hide! His glance swept onward, from side to side of the narrow street. A space so narrow—that Hannibal cannot follow!

But the storehouses that lined the way were built one against another. Hannibal was drawing near. Madoc could hear his heavy breathing.

The voice of the African called softly, "Stop, lad, stop!"

Madoc paid no heed. Just ahead, at the end of the street, he spied a vineyard. He could lose himself among the leafy vines! Hannibal's hand reached for him—fingertips brushed his shoulder. With a choking burst of speed, Madoc leaped toward his hiding place—so near he could see the tiny green grapes!

Again he felt Hannibal's reaching fingers at his shoulder. Madoc swerved and jerked free. Then suddenly he tripped. The earth rushed toward him as he plunged forward and crashed headlong into the pavement. The sole of a sandal, broken from its worn strap, flapped about his ankle.

Hannibal, unable to check himself, leaped over the fallen boy, then turned and caught him by the arm. Madoc lay still. Gasping and stunned, he felt no pain from his bruised arms and legs. He knew only that his plan had failed.

Now, nothing mattered. Nothing but hatred for the red-faced farmer who, at that moment, came puffing up behind him. Hatred for the African slave, hatred for the Romans, and for the whole world. He knew that Hannibal loosed his arm. Then he was caught by the back of the neck and jerked to his feet.

Madoc held out his hands in wild appeal. "Master, I pray you—"

"Silence!" roared the man, still holding Madoc's neck in a numbing grip. "You—you would dare to run away!" He was breathing hard. "Are you too stupid to understand that your body is no longer your own?"

He shook Madoc like a worried rabbit. "Do you not know that for trying to escape you may be beaten—and beaten again, until you cannot beg for mercy?"

Madoc mumbled frantically, "But hear, my lord, I pray you! I would not beg for mercy! I ask only that—"

Gratus' breath hissed through his clenched teeth. His free hand came down against Madoc's mouth in a crushing blow. "Son of a barbarian, I see you must be taught! A slave speaks only when he is spoken to!"

A final blow to the face, then he added, "Remember that, if you would live!"

Madoc limped back along the way he had come. He was not at all sure that he wanted to live. Hannibal supported him, holding his arm in a gentle but unbreakable grip. Madoc wiped the blood from his battered mouth with the back of his hand. The sandal that had betrayed him dragged along the pavement. It made a dull, scuffing sound.

The farmer looked back, scowling. "Take it off."

"I do it, lad," Hannibal whispered, and he stooped to undo the worn strap.

Gratus led them into the town, along the street of shops. They entered a long stone bazaar with a high arched roof and little booths opening into the center walk.

At the sound of a hammer striking on metal, Madoc lifted his head. A silversmith was working at his anvil. A metal bowl of glowing coals stood on the stone floor beside him. Madoc could see that he was hammering out a bracelet. Once upon a time, Madoc recalled, his mother had worn a bracelet of hammered silver on her arm. He remembered that it had been etched in the likeness of leaves from the sacred oak. Once again his eyes ached with unshed tears.

They passed the booth of a basket maker, sitting cross-legged at his work, his fingers moving faster than the eye could follow. At the lantern maker's booth just beyond, a row of brass lanterns hung on a long pole. They caught and reflected the afternoon sunshine that streamed into the bazaar from arched windows high above the shops.

"Pretty!" Hannibal whispered, pointing.

Madoc scarcely heard.

Gratus had stopped at the shop where the articles of leather were displayed. "A pair of sandals for the slave," he ordered.

The leather worker came with heavy cowhide and shears. He measured Madoc's feet on the leather, cut the sandals, and stitched the straps to the soles. It took only a few minutes.

"Put them on," snapped the farmer.

With a choked groan, Madoc forced his swollen feet into the stiff new sandals and fastened the straps about his ankles.

Next, they went to the public bath reserved for slaves and the very poor. It was a small pool in a shed-like, badly lighted building. Madoc had bathed only in icy mountain streams, and he found the water pleasantly warm. It brought some relief to the pain in his skinned arms and legs. He washed the blood from his bruised mouth and scrubbed his very dirty body.

An attendant cut short his mop of tangled hair. Another brought a clean tunic of coarse brown cloth to replace the tattered garment he had worn. His plaid cloak was of fine, heavy wool. His mother had woven it for him, long ago. He was thankful that it was not taken from him.

Now they trudged back to the street of the warehouses. Midway to the vineyard, Gratus stopped. He took from his belt a huge iron key that hung by a leather string and unlocked a storeroom. Then he handed to each of the slaves a piece of bread.

"What is your name?" he asked the African.

"Hannibal, if you please, my lord."

The farmer grinned with a downward turn of the lips. "You have taken the name of a great warrior. Your new master doubtless would be pleased to have him as a slave."

Once again Madoc was required to give his name. He watched as both names were written down on a bit of papyrus. Then the two were ordered inside, and Gratus shut and locked the door.

There was one high, slit-like window beside the door. By its light, Madoc could see that the room was partly filled with crates and boxes and bales of cloth. In one corner was a flattened pile of straw. He and Hannibal sat down on it.

The African ate his bread noisily and with apparent content. Madoc stared up at the narrow window, dull-eyed. The generous piece of coarse dark bread lay forgotten in his hand.

"Don't ever try to run away again, lad," Hannibal advised. He finished his bread and searched through the straw for crumbs.

"Don't even try, because there's no place for slaves to run to. All the world belongs to Rome."

He rocked back and forth as he sat cross-legged. His voice, deep and rich, was like water flowing over smooth stones. "All the world, lad, all the world belongs to Rome! Your land, my land, everybody's land!"

The slurred chanting of that friendly voice broke something loose in Madoc's chest. He flung himself face downward. Great sobs wrenched his tired body, and thawing tears dripped into the straw.

Hannibal made no move to stop him. "Lie still and rest, lad," he murmured. "And don't try to run away, ever again."

Madoc burst out, "I knew I could not hope to escape now, though someday I shall! But for today, if I could have had a little time—even an hour of freedom—"

Madoc's whole body drew up into a tight ball of pain. He pounded the straw with clenched fists. "I should not have minded a beating! I think—I should not have minded—even to die!"

Gradually his sobs grew fainter, while Hannibal rocked and chanted. Madoc heard him, as if from a long way off. At last he fell asleep, each breath ending in a tired hiccup.

At the first light of dawn, Madoc awoke with a start. His whole body ached, and his stomach called loudly for food. For a moment he lay still. Hannibal, sprawled across the straw, was still breathing deeply. Madoc sat up and looked for the bread he had dropped the night before. The faint crackle of straw roused the African. He stretched and yawned, then grinned as he saw Madoc eating his bread with real appetite.

"Farmer come pretty soon and take us to the farm," he said. His grin faded at the thought.

Madoc replied, "It must be a long way from the city, or he would have taken us there last night."

Hannibal nodded gloomily.

They listened to passing footsteps on the pavement outside. At last came the rumble of heavy wheels that stopped before their door. The iron key turned in the lock, and the door creaked open.

Gratus eyed them grimly as they got to their feet. He handed to each a piece of bread and a handful of ripe figs. As they ate, he said, "Bring the goods from the storeroom and pack them into the wagons. First the boxes, then the bales and smaller bundles."

Madoc stuffed the last of his breakfast into his mouth and hurried to do as he was told. Soon the clumsy ox-drawn cart was lumbering along the highway toward the east. Madoc walked with Hannibal beside the plodding oxen, while Gratus sat at ease on top of the load.

The sun was high and hot above their heads when they passed through a town. Gratus called them to halt before an open wine shop. Madoc glared with hatred at the farmer's retreating back, then sat down in the dust with Hannibal.

Coming toward them along the narrow street was a covered litter. It was carried on poles that were laid across the shoulders of two powerful servants. Madoc stared at the bold dark eyes and shining hair of the woman who sat in the shaded comfort of the litter, then at the sweating backs of her slaves. When he looked away, he licked his own battered lips and his mouth was bitter with hatred.

After a time Gratus came out and they went on. Madoc turned a dull eye upon the farmers who worked in the vineyards and vegetable gardens along the highway. A boy, too small to know the difference between slave and freeman, offered him a plump carrot with flakes of soil clinging to it. Madoc turned away.

That night he and Hannibal were locked in the crowded, ill-smelling slave quarters of a village inn. There they were free to talk in whispers, but Madoc ate and slept with no word for anyone.

Each day took on the pattern of the one before. But on the fourth day, Hannibal lifted his head and sniffed. "Must be coming to water. Smell the fresh cool air." He drew a deep breath. "Makes me think of home," he whispered. "The good smell of the lakes."

The bullwhip sang out, and Hannibal ducked. Madoc looked up. There was no water in sight, only the walls and tiled roofs of a large city. That night they lay in a dungeon-like room beneath a crowded inn.

"Hannibal," Madoc asked, "do you know where we are?"

After a thoughtful pause, the African answered. "Baker man used to talk about getting wheat from a town where ships came in. Said they brought it from lands far across the sea. It was toward the rising sun. Called the place Ancona."

Suddenly he sat up. "Lad! Hope the new master does not live beyond the sea!" He shuddered. "When you're on the ship and the shore slips away and there's nothing but water all around—"

It was the first time since leaving the warehouse at Cremona that Hannibal had worried about anything. Now he added in a hollow whisper, "Seems as if the gods can't find you when you've left the land. Waves come slapping against the boat, reaching for the poor slaves chained inside!"

Madoc, too, shuddered at the thought of crossing the sea. His dash for an hour's freedom had failed when a sandal strap broke and tripped him. That had been only a part of his plan. But how could he hope to carry out the rest of it if he were taken across the sea? It was a blow far more crushing than Gratus' fist had dealt him. Madoc slept little that night.

On the following day, Madoc caught his first glimpse of the sea as the morning mists rolled back and the sun shone through. But its beauty was lost to him.

"Hannibal" he muttered, "it is too much!"

"Too much what, lad?"

"Water! See how it moves up, wave on wave, like a Roman army marching to meet us?"

Hannibal nodded gloomily. "Wait till you get out there! The waves start lifting and pulling at the ship, trying to drag it under."

At the wharf, Gratus ordered them to stop. "Unload," he said, "and wait beside the cart."

Madoc drew a deep sigh of relief as the farmer hurried off. For the moment, he was free of chains and the hated eye of the Roman. He looked quickly to the right and left, but Hannibal's watchful eye was upon him. And Hannibal's words had sunk deep into his mind. Now they made a mournful song, timed to the surge of the incoming tide. "My land, your land, all the world belongs to Rome!"

Suddenly the African cried out and pointed seaward. A ship, coming from the south, was riding in on the tide.

"It's like a great white bird!" Madoc breathed. "A bird with the head and neck of a swan. And the curling waves on either side are like gleaming white wings!"

Now he could see the long, graceful oars that swept through the water—rising, pausing, falling again. As the ship came nearer, he heard a strange, muffled throbbing in perfect time with the dip of the oars. The heartbeat of the giant bird that was sweeping toward them!

All at once the throbbing stopped, and Madoc could see men hurrying about on deck. The square white sail was furled. The oars moved back again, and the ship headed straight for the stone wharf.

"Hannibal," Madoc cried, "it's going to crash upon the rocks!"

The African only grumbled unhappily in reply. Madoc waited and watched. Now—just one more dip of the oars and the wooden prow would be ground to splinters! He shrank back with hunched shoulders and narrowed eyes to await the crash.

Then again he leaned forward. The oars had stopped. They seemed to be pulling on one side, pushing on the other. The ship quivered, hesitated, then swung about in a rush of foaming green water. In a minute it settled gently against the wharf.

Madoc breathed in a noisy gasp.

Ropes were thrown ashore, and the ship was tied securely. Men on board leaped to the wharf, each to his task. Other men ran out to help. Empty casks were rolled from the deck; filled casks were taken aboard.

"Water," Hannibal explained. "Can't drink from that salty old ocean."

Madoc saw great sacks of grain tossed from the arms of one man to another as lightly as if they were filled with straw. He watched baskets of vegetables, and kegs of wine, and crates of live fowl taken on board.

Hannibal grumbled, "Working fast to load that ship. Must be we going out with the turn of the tide."

We? Madoc had almost forgotten. Now his eyes dulled as he saw Gratus hurrying from the wine shop where he had refreshed himself. The farmer wiped his mouth on his sleeve, then went to speak to the ship's captain. Madoc could not hear, but he saw Gratus point first to the pile of boxes and bales, then to the slaves who waited beside the pile.

The unhappy African groaned. "Pray, lad, pray!" His frightened gaze was fixed upon the two men. "If the gods don't help us right now, we are surely going away in that ship!"

Madoc shook his head. "I cannot pray! In my land, only the priests may speak to the gods. And even if I might call upon them, they could not hear my voice, far away in a strange land."

He glanced up at Hannibal's sagging chin. "Surely you know the gods of Rome. They are near at hand. Perhaps they would listen."

Hannibal shook his head. "Only to the Romans. They care not for slaves—poor helpless slaves that don't want to leave the land."

CHAPTER 3: STORM AT SEA

For his own safety, Madoc was not so much concerned. He knew that Gratus was not their owner but had bought Hannibal and himself for a centurion whom he called Cornelius. He knew that a centurion was an officer in the Roman army, the captain of a hundred men. Madoc had decided that Cornelius must be a soldier in some strange land that the Romans had conquered, far across the sea, and that he and Hannibal were to be shipped to him there.

Madoc's experience with Roman soldiers had not been happy. With Gratus, too, it had been bitter. He saw Gratus give to the captain a thin roll of papyrus. A list, no doubt, of the goods to be taken aboard. "At least," he muttered to Hannibal, "it would seem that the farmer is not going with us."

But the African was not to be cheered. He was still chanting sadly, "Don't want to leave the good hard earth! Don't want to get on that ship!"

"Be still," Madoc advised. "The ship came safely from a far land. Can it not return as well?"

Gratus turned and shouted, "Bring the goods to the ship's side!"

In spite of the low rumbling in Hannibal's throat, he did his part. He carried the baggage to the side of the ship and piled it along with other merchandise waiting to be stowed in the hold.

Suddenly and without warning, Madoc was seized by a husky hand and hustled aboard. In another minute he was tumbled down a steep flight of stairs. He landed in a place that was dark and evil-smelling. Hannibal, wailing loudly, came close behind. Then both were chained by the ankle to huge staples driven into one of the pillars that supported the deck above them.

Madoc made no sound as he stared straight before him. His eyes were black with hatred for every hand that touched him, for every careless look that said, "You are nothing—a slave."

As his eyes became accustomed to the gloom, he noticed a number of men resting on a pile of straw. They, too, were chained. They paid no attention to the men who ran up and down the stairs, stowing away merchandise. He and Hannibal were, he knew, a part of that merchandise.

Madoc leaned back against the post to which he was chained. He looked down at the iron band about his ankle. "In truth, Hannibal, our bodies belong to the men who made these chains." Then he straightened. "But there is something inside that still belongs to us."

He closed his eyes as he tried to make his meaning clear in his own mind. Hannibal, still moaning, was not even listening. "Something that the bullwhip cannot reach," Madoc went on. "In my land there is a god, a ruler over all the others. The druids, who are the priests of my people, call him Mabon. The

Romans have tried to make us believe that he is the same as their god, Jupiter. But many do not believe that." Madoc's eyes flashed open. "I do not believe it! I want nothing that is of Rome!"

Hannibal was not impressed. He shook his head from side to side. "Don't care what you call him. Just need a god to take care of us now."

The hold was becoming more and more crowded. Only a small space was left for the chained men. The noise overhead became deafening as bars of iron from the mines of Gaul were taken aboard.

At last, all was quiet. Then the ship began to rock with the tide. Madoc was startled by a thunderous boom from the hold itself. He had paid no attention to the activity about him. Now he saw that some of the chained men had been loosed and driven to the oars. They were seated on benches along both sides of the ship, three to an oar. Another boom and Madoc looked up to a balcony in the stern, where a ship's officer was seated. Through an opening high up in the front of the hold, the man at the drum could see the helmsman on the deck. And by its light, he was able to watch the men at the oars.

As Madoc watched, the man struck the mallet against a drum in front of him. At the sound of the drum, the men bent to their oars.

"Now," said Madoc aloud, "I understand!"

Gone from his mind was the picture of the great white

bird with the beating heart. He listened and watched. Boom, boom—boom! Lift, pause—lower, pull!

Slowly and smoothly the ship began to move.

Hannibal's dark eyes opened round and wide as it scraped against the wharf, then rode free. "Lad, lad," he whispered huskily, "somewhere there must be a god that listens to slaves chained in the dark insides of ships! I'm going to pray!"

Madoc was not listening. His attention was fixed on the men at the oars. He noted the bulging muscles of their shoulders and arms. He watched the swing of their naked bodies, all in perfect time with the drum. As if each, he decided, was a part of the ship's great body.

He turned next to study the faces of the men near him. Only one had fair skin and blue eyes. A few had dark hair and eyes, but their features were not those of the proud Romans. The rest were of Hannibal's race. And yet, thought Madoc, there is something alike about all of them!

By the light from the stairway, Madoc watched and wondered. The day drew to a close. Oil lamps, hung by chains from the low ceiling, were lighted by a man carrying a torch on the end of a pole.

The men at the oars were released, and others went to take their places. As the tired slaves passed on their way to rest, suddenly Madoc knew why they all seemed alike. Only their bodies were alive! One and all, their faces had died!

Madoc's eyes grew dull as he muttered aloud, "I, too, am a slave!"

That night Madoc dreamed of his homeland. He was fleeing through the forest from a drove of wild boars. One of his feet seemed weighted—so heavy he could scarcely lift it. The boars were nearly upon him. He glanced back, saw their long, cruel tusks as they leaped forward to bear him down. He strained at his weighted leg. Then he awoke with a start. His heart was pounding, and he was breathing hard. He sat up in a panic, and the iron band dragged at his ankle.

To clear the dream from his mind, Madoc looked about. The air was thick with smoke from the sputtering lamps. Through the haze he could make out the bodies of the galley slaves, moving woodenly back and forth to the beat of the drum. Hannibal was sleeping soundly.

Madoc thought again of home. He recalled how he had once snared a crested wren, the bird most sacred to the priestly druids. To kill it for food would have been a sin. But he had held it in his two hands and felt the beating of its tiny heart. It had not struggled or made any outcry until, still holding its feet, he had released its wings. Then it had pecked fiercely at his wrist, drawing blood. It had beaten the air with its wings until it was exhausted and hopeless. Finally, he had opened his fingers and watched as the wren soared away into the treetops.

"How that bird must have hated me!" he muttered to himself. But the wren had been foolish, fighting against so strong a foe. Madoc's body stiffened. "I will wait," he vowed. "I will not give up, as the men at the oars have done."

He lay down and closed his eyes. One day he would steal away. Far, far out of reach of the chains that held him now. And his mother—somehow, sometime, he would come back across the sea to her.

Early the next morning a guard came down the steps. To Madoc's surprise, his leg iron was unfastened.

"Get up," said the guard. "You are to attend to the need of the others."

Madoc's heart thrilled. Was this the chance he had dreamed of in the night, coming so soon?

His good sense told him at once that it was not. Though he had learned to swim like one of the beavers in the ponds near his home, he would have no chance for life among the waves of the sea.

Madoc followed the guard back up the steps. He would wait. He would lie quietly, as the wren had done at first. And when his moment arrived, he would make no mistake.

The guard pointed out a large canvas sack that lay on the deck. "There is bread. Take a loaf to each of the galley slaves, and one for yourself and the African." His heavy dark brows drew closer as he warned, "Mind you, no talking, and only one to each. The loaves are counted."

In the days that followed, Madoc listened and learned. They were going to a land called Judea. The journey would take about five weeks, if the gods sent favorable winds. And every morning Madoc watched as an offering was made on deck to win their favor.

The captain had just sprinkled salt and barley on the altar when, a few days later, Madoc glimpsed a rocky beach close by to the north. Back of it were towering wooded hills. He had filled a basket with bread for the slaves in the hold. Now his heart quickened as he glanced about. Every eye was upon the captain who stood with thick palms lifted as he begged the favor of fair winds. Madoc moved to the rail. He could let himself over the side. With care, there need be no sound as he dropped into the water. And there was a quiet little inlet among the rocks where one could swim ashore.

He set his basket down beside him. His pounding heart drowned out the rush of the waves, the sound of the captain's prayers.

"Thinking of leaving the ship?" growled a voice at his elbow. Madoc jumped. He whirled about.

The black-browed guard was grinning. "Your child's body would be crushed like an egg upon the rocks," he sneered.

A blow to the shoulder tumbled Madoc to the deck. "Go below and stay until you are called."

As he picked up his basket, a vicious kick sent him reeling toward the stairs. The moldy black loaves flew in every direction. Madoc gathered them hastily, knowing that the man was watching every move.

He was no smarter than the wren had been, Madoc mused. Even his thoughts had betrayed him. As soon as he was out of sight from the deck, his smoldering hatred burst into words. "But they cannot chain my thoughts," he muttered. "And when my body is free, every blow will be remembered."

When the bread had been distributed, Madoc sat down beside Hannibal. The African glanced up. "You look angry, lad."

"And for good reason," Madoc replied. "I have been chained and beaten and driven! I may not even speak to my mother before I am hustled aboard this ship! And now I am kicked because I look across the water and think of her!"

"Your mother, lad? Where is she?"

"Right here in Cremona! I saw the weaver's mill, where she is a slave. We passed it on the way to the slave market. I could have circled back through the vineyard and found her there if the sandal strap had not broken! And now the ship takes me farther and farther away!" His face blazed with sudden fury. "There is not room in my mind for anything but anger and hatred!"

Hannibal nodded, then closed his eyes. His body swayed from side to side as he mumbled a strange jungle chant. Gradually Madoc's thoughts grew quiet, though his ribs still ached where the kick had landed.

"Hannibal," he said, "wouldn't you like to go back to your homeland?"

The African swallowed quickly. "Just was thinking about that. And the lake with the fish in it. Wishing for some of that tender white fish meat."

He told Madoc about his mother, and about the jungle village where wild beasts came boldly to the huts of his people.

Madoc asked, "Had you no gods to protect you?"

Hannibal's brow wrinkled. "Don't know as you could call them gods. Good spirits in the woods, but we gave them little thought. Had to be friendly with the bad spirits to keep them from doing us harm."

Madoc watched the oarsmen as he ate his small portion of coarse unsalted bread. When he had finished, he asked, "But Hannibal, if you have no gods, who was the god you prayed to the day we left the land?"

Hannibal grinned. "Don't know," he confessed. "Just prayed."

His smile widened as he met Madoc's questioning eyes. "Must be somebody is taking care of Hannibal. All this water pitching and tossing the ship around and not getting me wet. Next time things look bad for us, lad, you pray, too."

Not many days later Madoc, coming down from the deck, told Hannibal that black clouds were gathering and the wind was rising. The eyes of the chained man widened in fear.

The wind increased. The sail was lowered, but the drum boomed on at a steady tempo. The galley slaves strained at their oars. Their faces looked gray and fearful as they watched the man on the balcony.

The heavy-browed guard lurched down the stairs. Madoc was chained, and as a huge wave broke against the prow, a surge of panic passed over him. Now the ship's life was his life.

Hannibal's head rolled unhappily, and the oarsmen were nearly thrown from their seats. The prow lifted steeply, then dived from crest to trough of the mighty swell. Madoc's stomach seemed to climb up into his throat. He closed his eyes and leaned hard against the solid oak of the post at his back.

"Can't even pray," Hannibal moaned. "Just have to trust god to do what he knows I need."

The wind howled down the stairs. Little jets of spray whipped in at the leather-bound holes through which the oars extended downward at an angle into the sea. A few drops dashed against Madoc's clenched hand, and he opened his eyes. He licked off the water. Its salty tang was pleasant to his tongue.

He could see the faces and shoulders of the oarsmen shining with sweat. Their chests heaved. The guard, whip in hand, walked back and forth as best he could in the pitching ship, between the rows of laboring slaves.

As he watched, Madoc's fears were drowned in a rising tide of anger. "There is no need of the whip," he shouted, knowing that his voice was hidden by the roar of the storm. "Dog of a Roman, can you not see that the men are giving every beat of their hearts?"

Then suddenly the blue-eyed oarsman collapsed. Like a tired child, his body folded down against the man next to him.

The guard's whip sang out and struck. For a moment it clung about the slave's naked shoulders. Then it lifted, leaving behind a long, blood-red welt. The man screamed. He raised his head and clutched at his place on the oar.

Madoc leaped to his feet. He beat his fists against the oaken pillar and flung his arms about it as the ship rolled. "May the fury of all the gods of Gaul rest upon you," he shouted at the man with the whip. "May the evil spirits of Hannibal's land torment you! May the vengeance of any god whose name I know not, be visited upon you!"

The ship settled into a moment of rocking calm, and Madoc's voice sank to a cautious growl. "May you be cursed with all the pain you have brought to the others! You and all the sons of Rome!"

The vessel shuddered with another blast. A crash of splintering timber above and water poured down the steps.

Hannibal leaped to his feet with a scream. Madoc watched, fascinated. The stream bounced from step to step, then it splashed to the floor in a swirling pool. Hannibal wrapped both arms about the pillar to which they were chained and lifted first one foot and then the other. His face was twisted in panic.

Another blast shook the tormented vessel. It spun sidewise. Then, suddenly, silence. The only sound that could make itself heard above the roar of the storm was stilled. The pulse of the drum had stopped!

Madoc glanced up. The drummer had been flung from his seat, and the startled galley slaves had lost the beat. Madoc saw them strain in confusion. Then with one accord, they fell forward against their oars for a moment of gasping relief.

But it was over in the space of a few quickened heartbeats.
The drummer regained his seat and the drum boomed
commandingly. Every oar was poised, every head raised—save
one. The man with the red welt across his shoulders!

Madoc watched as the guard rushed forward. The whip
snapped out. It curled again and again, and the body of the
blue-eyed slave jerked in agony. Thin hands clawed at the oar,
but the man's head rolled helplessly.

Madoc's stomach heaved. He tried to shout, but his breath
stopped and the words choked in his throat.

The ship righted itself, then suddenly dipped again.
Shuddering and sick, Madoc lowered his eyes. The water that
had been sloshing about at his feet was now rushing forward
in a low crested wave. When it reached the feet of the guard,
Madoc saw him slip. His body spun like a top. The long whip,
swinging above his head, jerked back with the snap of a striking
snake to curl about his own face. It stuck and clung, then loosed
itself as the man staggered and fell, his face twisted in a scream
of pain.

Madoc jumped up with a smothered cry, then slumped to
the floor and buried his face in his hands. His shoulders heaved.

In a moment a hand was on his arm and Hannibal's worried
voice close to his ear. "Don't cry, lad! Poor old ship may yet live
through!"

Madoc looked up through streaming tears. "I—crying? Oh,
Ha-Hannibal, you did not see? Look—look at the guard, there

on the floor! See the bleeding red welt across his ugly mouth! Around the bull's neck!"

Madoc screamed again with crazy laughter. "I—crying? Never!"

Hannibal mumbled in panic, "Hush, lad, hush! Seems like old guard's looking right this way!"

But it did not matter, for Madoc's face was again hidden.

In a few minutes, Madoc lifted his head and mopped the tears from his cheeks with the sleeve of his tunic. He saw the guard, still seated on the wet floor, rocking in pain. Then he looked at his countryman. Once again the man was pulling weakly in time with the others.

Madoc drew a long quivering breath. "Hannibal," he announced in a solemn tone, "the wind is going down. I think the storm is over."

CHAPTER 4: A NEW COUNTRY

They stopped at an island port for the ship to be repaired. Though once again he was chained, Madoc was thankful that the galley slaves were permitted to rest.

"Consider, Hannibal," he said when the ship was again underway, "how much more fortunate we are than the men at the oars. Think what it would mean to know we never could leave this ill-smelling place. Never see the land, or watch the sun come up. Just go on and on, from bed to oar and back again until—"

He did not finish. One of the galley slaves groaned as he turned on his bed of rough straw. It was the man who had been beaten during the storm. There was no one about, save the officer on the balcony. His attention was fixed upon the oarsmen and the man at the helm.

Madoc got up, thankful that once again his leg iron had been unfastened. He crept to the water cask that stood in a nearby corner. Quickly he dipped a cup and carried it to his countryman. Staring at Madoc, the man took the cup with shaking hands and drank. Then he whispered in the Gallic tongue, "May the spirits of the forest protect you, my son."

Madoc's face lit up. He muttered in reply, "And may the mistletoe bring healing to your wounds."

Slave Boy in Judea

He dared say no more. As he moved away, he glanced back. The man was smiling. His eyes were fixed upon the oaken beams above him, as if in them he saw the leafy forests of his homeland.

It was more than a week later that the quiet was broken by the sound of running feet on deck. Then came the cry of "Land! Land!"

There were shouted orders. The guard came down the stairs. He fastened Madoc's leg iron. When he had gone, Hannibal grinned hopefully. "They lowering the sail, lad. Maybe we going to get off this ship."

They waited. Finally, there came a quickening in the beat of the drum that sent the ship skimming forward. Hannibal gathered his legs under him and strained against his chain. But his mood was gloomy.

"Never did belong to a soldier. Don't like their swords and battle-axes." He shuddered. "Don't like those long pointed lances."

Madoc muttered, "It's the man I hate, rather than the sword and lance."

He stopped speaking to watch and listen. He saw the muscles bulge in the arms of the galley slaves as the oars on the right were held. The ship quivered, then took a slow turn. For a moment it heaved in the trough of the waves. Next, he felt a bumping and scraping as it settled into quiet water against a stone wharf.

Madoc's body stiffened. He heard the confusion of unloading, then footsteps close above on the stairs. The ship's captain came first, his fat paunch shaking with every step. Two Roman soldiers followed. One of them carried a sword, but Madoc was sure that neither was of the rank of centurion.

With a greasy finger, the captain pointed out boxes and bales and, last of all, Hannibal and Madoc. "All these," he said, "belong to Cornelius the centurion."

The two slaves were released. Hannibal stretched his legs. Then he picked up two of the heaviest boxes and started up the steps. Madoc hoisted a bale of cloth to his shoulder and followed.

The man with the sword shouted after them, "Place the goods on the wharf, and wait beside them!"

As more merchandise was moved from the ship, a small man in a loose gray mantle came to stand beside them. He wore a white cap, bound around with a fold of yellow cloth. He looked at Madoc with lifted eyebrows and wrinkled forehead, as if he were surprised or worried. When he turned his head, Madoc noticed that his right ear, like Hannibal's, had been pierced by an awl. He shuddered. Would he be branded in the same way?

When everything had been unloaded and checked, the baggage was gathered up by the three slaves and hired burden bearers. They followed the soldiers along the wharf to the town. Madoc, looking toward the north, saw a flat cliff overhanging the sea. On its top was a castle of white stone. That, he thought, would be the home of the city's Roman ruler.

He glanced back at the ship they had just left. It was no longer beautiful to him, as when he had seen it first. In his mind's eye, he was looking down now into the dark heart of it, where wretched men lay on filthy beds of straw, chained and hopeless.

Then Madoc thought again of his mother. She, too, sat chained to her task with no hope of release. His lips grew tight. Someday his chance would come. He would slip aboard a ship like that. Hide amid the freight it carried, and return to set her free. He looked up at the strange faces all about him, then sighed and put away his dreams.

Madoc and Hannibal walked behind the gray-clad slave along a narrow street where men paused in their noisy bargaining to watch the strange procession. Suddenly a sad, long-faced camel came lurching and growling toward them.

"Step aside!" shouted one of the soldiers. Madoc lost no time in crowding his body against the stone wall of a shop.

A mother dog, coarse-haired and thin, lay in the middle of the street with three tiny puppies. Madoc cried out in alarm lest the strange beast tread upon them. But somehow the camel's huge padded feet avoided the homeless little family.

The procession came in a short time to the city's wide arched gateway. There a blind man lay begging in the shade. Nearby a group of bearded old men in long mantles of many colors stood talking loudly in a language that was strange to Madoc.

"Jews," whispered Hannibal.

The soldiers pushed through the group. The old men stepped aside, casting ugly glances after the Romans.

Coming out into the sunshine again, Madoc found himself in the farmers' marketplace. A merchant in a long greasy mantle was dipping olive oil from a big open jar to the leather bottle of a customer. Between the booths of the traders a man led a small rough-haired donkey, laden with skins of wine, toward the city gates.

The paved road led to the east up a gradual slope, through a street of homes. Madoc caught glimpses of white houses with tiled roofs and gardens about them. Strange trees waved fanlike fronds over the high stone walls.

The white houses, he was sure, were the homes of Romans. They were like the villas he had seen in Italy—so different from the thatched log houses of his own land.

The party stopped before the door of a large villa. One of the soldiers pulled the knocker. A small sharp-eyed serving woman admitted them. As he stepped inside, Madoc stared in amazement at tinted walls and brightly tiled floor. Through a doorway to the right he could see porches with high pillars and walks that enclosed a courtyard. On his left were more porches and a walled garden.

When the baggage had been counted again and the hired burden bearers dismissed, Madoc and Hannibal were called into a small room at the rear of the house. The man with the sword took from the front of his tunic the much-fingered roll of papyrus. He looked it over carefully.

"What is your name?" he asked the African.

"Hannibal, if it please my lord."

The man nodded. "And yours?"

Madoc's answer was one brief word. The soldier frowned but said nothing.

He turned to the serving woman. "Show these slaves where they are to sleep. Send them to the bath, then give them something to eat."

He added to his companion, "Those cargo ships are as filthy as rats' nests. The smell of that hold is still in my nose. And, judging from the look of these two, they have had little enough to eat."

As he turned to leave, he looked the two slaves up and down. Then he grinned. "Our captain should have no difficulty in telling them apart," he said to his companion. "Have you ever seen such an ill-matched pair?"

Madoc glanced up. Hannibal's huge body was slouched a little at the shoulders. His white teeth gleamed in a good-natured grin.

The other man replied, "The African is as beautiful as a lazy tiger. And the lad, with his blue eyes and yellow hair—" he interrupted himself to laugh aloud—"perhaps the centurion will wear him as an ornament on his breastplate."

They went out of the door, still laughing. Madoc flushed with anger, but he kept his eyes lowered until the door closed.

He followed Hannibal and the serving woman through the
courtyard. They walked past a tiled pool, in the middle of which
was a pedestal. A marble cherub, with legs wide apart, stood
on the pedestal. He was pouring water into the pool from a
pitcher that was nearly as large as his own fat little body. Madoc
grinned faintly.

Bees hummed about the fruit of a tree that was laden with
glossy black mulberries, and Madoc could hear sparrows
twittering among the thick green leaves.

The woman pointed to the doorway of a tiny room at the
rear of the yard. Madoc and Hannibal entered.

In a very few minutes, the manservant with the lifted
eyebrows came. He brought a clean tunic for Madoc, a loincloth
for Hannibal. Then he led them back to the city gates and on
to a small low building on a side street. There, in an unheated
pool, they washed. Madoc came out with his skin tingling, his
short hair curling close to his head, and a terrific hunger in his
stomach.

Back at the villa, they were given a supper of bread and meat
and sun-dried figs. When they had finished, Hannibal sighed
with satisfaction. But Madoc muttered, "It is much too good
to last. We must remember that our master is a Roman and a
soldier."

He sat down in the doorway of their little room. On three
sides the courtyard was enclosed by covered walks. The rooms
of the villa lay beyond.

Twilight was deepening. Madoc watched the awl-marked servant light with a long taper the bronze lamps that hung above the walks. When all were lighted and the slave had gone away, Madoc turned.

"Hannibal," he asked softly, "have you heard the name of this city to which we have come?"

But Hannibal was asleep. Madoc lay down beside him on a bed of straw.

He awoke the next morning with a start. He sat up with the same sense of panic that he had felt so many times since the Romans first fastened the iron bands about his wrists—the morning he started on the long march to the slave market.

He got up quietly, so as not to waken Hannibal. He stepped to the doorway. No one was stirring; there was no smoke coming from the chimney above the kitchen. He slipped out and sidled along the wall until he came to a gate. It opened into a vegetable garden. In the barnyard back of the garden, chickens and geese were already about. They moved aside as the silent gray-clad figure crept through the yard. Through another gate Madoc went—a gate that led to open country.

The villa was built against a gentle slope. Behind it, as far as Madoc could see, rose other hills. They were dotted with small trees. He found a path, beaten hard by the hoofs of sheep and goats, and he raced away.

The bushes that brushed his legs were dripping with mist that had come in from the sea during the night. Finally he stopped, breathless and thrilled with the sense of freedom.

At the sound of hurrying feet on the path below, Madoc's heart leaped in choking fear. He strained his eyes to see through the mist. Then, above a tangle of brush, Hannibal's dark head came into view.

Madoc cried out, "Hannibal! Why are you here?"

The African grinned, as if he would apologize. He climbed up closer, then stopped to catch a few hurried breaths. "Remember how you tried to run away before, lad? I thought—I feared—I mean—you must not try again!"

"I told you, I was not trying to escape!" Madoc's voice was sharp. "I wanted only to see my mother. And someday, I shall!"

He caught himself from saying more by laying a hand on Hannibal's bare shoulder. "Listen to the song of the lark! It sounds just as it did in the hills near my village! And the sun is coming up—it is the same too!"

Hannibal agreed. "Same old sun. Never can get away from it." They watched as the golden disc widened above the eastern hill.

"In truth," Madoc exclaimed, "he is over all the world. Once my father told me that long ago our people worshiped the sun. He must be a good and powerful god."

Suddenly a breeze sprang up, and the fog lifted in ragged, swirling banners. Madoc turned and started back down the hill. The mist, still heavy on every weed and thorn, sparkled in the sunlight. Madoc's mood was almost gay.

As they neared the barnyard gate, he spoke softly. "I have decided, Hannibal, to worship Mabon, the sun-god of my forefathers. I have no sacrifice to offer, but every day when he appears I shall bow down and worship him."

He lowered his voice to a harsh whisper. "I shall ask him to return to the Romans equal hurt for the wrong they have done to me." Hannibal made no reply.

Madoc opened the gate. He paid no heed to the quacking and clucking of the fowl as he leaned for a moment against the stone fence. He looked up, full into the face of the god he had decided to worship. He added softly, "And I shall ask him, each time I pray, to help me to return to my mother."

He slipped through the garden gate into the courtyard just as the manservant came to call them.

The centurion did not return until afternoon. Madoc, working in the stable with Hannibal, heard the clatter of horses' feet against the stone-paved street. There were shouted orders, then a hostler led a single black horse around the outer wall of the garden to the barnyard.

"Brush him down," said the hostler, "and see that he has water and food."

They were still working when the serving woman came to call them. She looked at them sharply. "Take water to your room. Wash yourselves. Get the smell of the stable from your bodies."

When they were thoroughly scrubbed, she led them to the library. Madoc walked in first. He looked about uneasily, then lowered his eyes. Behind a small carved table sat the centurion.

His dark head was bent over the same dirty scroll of papyrus that Madoc had seen first in the hands of Gratus. In another quick glance, Madoc saw that the Roman had laid aside his breastplate. His forehead, damp with perspiration, showed a reddened line where the strap of his helmet had rubbed.

Madoc stopped a few steps from the door. He heard a worried sigh as Hannibal came to wait beside him.

The centurion looked up, frowning. He stared for a long moment at his new possessions. Madoc could hear Hannibal's calloused feet scratching uneasily on the tiled floor.

"Come nearer," barked the new master. "Hold up your heads."

He stared into their faces, then picked up his reed pen and dipped it into a small bronze inkwell. "I wish to know all about you, up to the time Gratus bought you in Cremona."

Hannibal was disposed of first. He had grown up, he told the centurion, in the lake country of Africa. Years ago, he had been captured by slave traders and taken to Carthage. From there he had been shipped to Italy. He told briefly of his two owners, the farmer and the baker.

"You will work in the stables or in the kitchen. Reuben the Jew and his wife, Anna, will tell you what to do," said the centurion.

Hannibal backed hastily from the room. His head was lowered, his hands folded across his chest as a sign of submission to the new master.

Cornelius wrote on the scroll, then looked up at Madoc.

"You are young to be in slavery," he said. His voice was sharp, as if the boy were in some way to blame. "I marvel that Gratus thought you strong enough to serve me. Yet"—he seemed now to be talking to himself—"he paid very little. The loss would be small if—"

He did not finish, but sat thinking. As he thought, he made dots and lines on a wax tablet that lay open beside the papyrus.

"Where is your father?" he asked so suddenly that Madoc jumped.

"My father—is not."

"How did he die?"

"He was slain in a quarrel with a Roman soldier over a deer that both claimed to have killed."

Cornelius wrote. Then he asked, "Your mother—what of her?"

Madoc hesitated. Dare he tell the thing, exactly as it had happened?

The centurion snapped, "Attend to my words! I expect the whole story!"

Madoc hesitated no longer. He flung back his head and spoke rapidly. "After my father was killed, my mother was called before the magistrate. She took with her, hidden in the folds of her cloak, an arrow from my father's quiver. It was exactly like the arrow that had been found in the heart of the deer. She showed it to the judge. She was trying to prove that my father had killed the deer. But the magistrate was angered by her boldness, and he sent her into slavery."

The metal stylus scratched more dots and lines into the wax. "And you?" Cornelius asked after a pause, "What happened to you?"

"I was not at home when my mother was taken. At her command I had fled to the woods before the soldiers came. For a month I lived alone in the forest."

Cornelius said, "Were you not afraid of the lions and wild boars?"

"I was not afraid," Madoc answered, "but I was hungry and cold and lonely. I wanted to learn what had befallen my mother. So I came back to sleep in the hut of an old woman whom my mother had befriended."

"How were you finally caught?"

"I was betrayed by one of my own village—a cowardly herdsman who sought to win favor with the Romans."

"You speak boldly for a slave." The centurion scowled even more darkly as he looked up. "Now be sure you tell the truth. What happened at the slave market? Gratus reports that you tried to escape."

Madoc's face flushed with anger so sudden that he forgot to be afraid. "That is not true, O master! I tried to explain to your servant, Gratus. I begged him to hear me, but he would not listen."

"What was it you wished to tell him?"

Madoc tried to keep his voice steady. "On the long march from my home to Cremona, I heard the guards talking of her—of my mother. They had taken her to the slave market there a month before. I heard one say that she was much too beautiful to be chained at the loom of Julius the weaver."

Cornelius did not interrupt. Madoc's voice was shaking and hoarse as he went on. "For all the rest of the journey, I lived only for the time when I might slip away—just long enough to go to the weaving mill. I thought—if I could see her—if only for a moment—"

Madoc stopped. When he spoke again, his voice came from his throat in a choked whisper in which there was no sound. Still, Cornelius did not look up. Still, he sat with his eyes fixed on the dots and lines he was making in the wax.

"I thought," Madoc tried again, "I thought I could go on—if I could but say to her a word or two! I thought I would not mind even if—even if it meant—"

He could not finish.

Cornelius concluded for him. "Even if it meant a beating, such as is given only to runaway slaves."

He looked up into Madoc's twitching face. It was streaked with tears. "Go now. Anna will tell you what to do."

Madoc backed away. His breath came in choking sobs. He forgot to fold his hands across his chest, but it did not matter.

His master had not bothered to look up again. Madoc groped his way blindly into the courtyard, past the gay little marble cherub, and stumbled into the tiny room at the rear.

He flung himself down upon his cloak and wept violently. How he hated the centurion! Hated him more than the slave traders who had driven him across the mountains! More than the auctioneer who had sold him, or the guard on the ship who had beaten his countryman! Hated him more, even, than Gratus and his bullwhip! For Cornelius had seen him cry! Madoc—the son of a Gallic warrior!

CHAPTER 5:
CORNELIUS, THE MASTER

On the following morning, Madoc lay thinking. He had
not told Cornelius of his final talk with his mother before she
was arrested. At that time he had vowed that, if she were sent
into slavery, he would find and free her. His plan to see her in
Cremona was only to repeat that he could come to free her and
take her back to Gaul.

He was soon called again to stand before his master.
Cornelius sat as before at the small table. "You will sleep in the
trundle bed that is pushed under mine," he told Madoc. "Anna
will give you a pad. Put it on your bed."

Madoc would be sorry to leave Hannibal, but he said
nothing.

"When I am at home," the centurion went on, "you will
attend me. Be ready to do my bidding at all times. You will go
with me to camp. There you will take care of my armor. Keep
my sword sharp and clean. I will send you to the barracks where
a soldier will teach you all that you need to know." His brows
drew close in a thoughtful frown. "For the present, I think I will
not have your ear marked with the awl."

Again the scroll of papyrus lay before him. Cornelius took up his pen. "You speak the language of Rome fairly well. How is that?"

Madoc replied, "Your tongue, O master, is spoken throughout all the villages of Gaul. I learned it along with the Gallic of my people."

Cornelius nodded. "Now you must learn Aramaic, the language of the people here in Judea. Reuben and Anna will help you. You will also learn to read and write. I shall hire a Greek freedman to teach you." He looked up sharply. "See that you do not waste your time."

Madoc bowed. He would have backed away, but Cornelius dipped his pen into the ink. "Yesterday you did not give me the name of your father."

"He was Duncan, a landowner of the tribe of the Salassi."

Cornelius wrote. "And your mother's name?"

"Greta, of the line of Brian, who was a chief among the Salassi before the coming of the Romans."

Madoc walked to the courtyard and on into the kitchen. He was bewildered by the things the master had said to him. He could understand that a man might want to know as much as possible about the parents of a slave, just as he would inquire concerning the breed of a horse or a hunting dog. But why should he plan to educate a slave? Why pay a teacher so that a slave might learn to read and write? And why was he not to be branded with the awl?

Anna led Madoc to the big reception hall. She showed him how to sweep the tiled floor with a feather broom, then scrub it with a sponge. In the middle of the room was a tile-lined pool and, just above, an oblong opening in the ceiling which laid a dazzling patch of sunlight on the water.

Madoc stood for a moment to gaze about the room. There were several backless chairs of wrought iron and two couches with beautifully carved legs and feather-filled pads. Sponge in hand, he stared at the wall paintings, the marble figures, and the rich draperies that served as doors. Then he went to work.

Suddenly Anna's sharp voice re-called him. "The master's lunch is ready," she told him as he entered the kitchen. "Clean yourself. Smooth your hair. It is sticking up like a broom. Hold the tray away from your body."

Once again Madoc found Cornelius in the library. The centurion was lying on a couch, his right leg lifted and bent over the left. He was writing on a pad that rested against his bent knee.

Madoc set a small three-legged table close beside the couch and placed the tray upon it.

Cornelius spoke without looking up. "Can you find your way back to the wharf from which you came yesterday?"

"Yes, my lord," Madoc answered as he placed silver plates of bread and cheese and fruit on the table.

Still, the centurion did not look up or stop writing. "Stand outside the door. In a few minutes these letters will be ready. I want you to deliver them to the captain of the ship on which you came."

Madoc backed to the doorway and waited outside. Anna brought him bread and cheese, which he ate hurriedly. Soon he was called by Cornelius' sharp handclap.

"Make all haste," ordered the centurion as he handed Madoc the letters and two coins. "The ship will probably sail at the turn of the tide."

Madoc hurried to the gate of the city and along the street of shops to the water. There bales of wool, strong smelling kegs of salted fish, and sacks of grain lay waiting to be loaded. In the shade of nearby warehouses, hired burden bearers lay at rest in the heat of the noonday. Madoc shaded his own flushed face with his forearm, for the reflection of the sun on the water blinded him.

He looked for the ship with the head of a swan at its prow. When he found it, he clambered aboard and asked to speak to the captain.

As he waited, Madoc looked at the dark well of the stairway that led down into the hold. He sniffed the sickening odor that arose from it and turned away. And yet, the ship was going back—crossing the sea that separated him from his mother! Suddenly his heart leaped with a jolt that shook his whole body. He could slip down those stairs and hide among the boxes and bales! He could use the money his master had sent with the letters to buy food at the first island port.

Madoc glanced about quickly. The sailors were all resting, sprawled on the deck, mantles drawn over their faces to shut out the sun. His heart pounded in his throat. Now—he could slip down! The galley slaves would all be resting, too. Even if they saw him, they would say nothing. And, once in Ancona, he knew every step of the way back to Cremona where his mother sat in her chains!

Suddenly he remembered the wren—beating its wings, just as his heart was hammering now! Why had the Roman sent him, instead of Rueben or Hannibal, to take the letters? Could it be that his master had chosen him purposely, to see if he would try to escape?

The captain, aroused from his rest in the shade, came forward. At sight of the slave boy, he growled, "You again? I thought I had seen the last of you!"

Madoc heard his own voice speaking, as if from far away. "My master Cornelius asks that you deliver these letters to the master of the mails at Ancona."

He handed over the letters. The captain's red face rocked before him as he held out the coins. "He bade me give you these."

The captain smiled widely as the two coins dropped into his greasy palm. "Ah, yes! The good centurion! In all Caesarea there is none so generous as he! Tell your master that I myself will deliver the letters without fail, if the gods bring us safely to port."

He studied the addresses. "Um-m. To Petronia, his wife, and to Gratus, the overseer of his farm near Cremona."

He tucked the letters away in a leather knapsack and ambled back to his place in the shade. There he lay down with a noisy yawn and closed his eyes.

With shaking knees Madoc walked to the ship's side and looked down. Tiny waves were lifting and pulling against the ropes that held the vessel to the wharf. The tide was running out. A last backward look, then he leaped ashore and walked away with bent head.

As he entered the shade of the city gate, Madoc turned and looked back suddenly. He caught a glimpse of a white-and-yellow headdress as a little man with lifted eyebrows ducked out of sight.

He was right! Cornelius had sent the worried little Jew to spy upon him! Madoc's chin lifted. He drew a long deep sigh of relief and walked on.

Arriving at the villa, he went around to the barnyard gate and through the courtyard. He glanced into the library. He wanted to tell his master that the letters were safe aboard the ship. The room was empty, but he could hear voices coming from the walled garden on the far side of the villa. He walked through the house and waited on the porch, beside a pillar. He could see Cornelius talking to a white-haired man whose thin hands were clasped about a bundle of yellowed parchment scrolls. His master's voice was sharp. The old man's was quiet, though firm.

"You, Orestes," shouted the centurion, "a man of much learning—to forsake in your old age the gods of your people for a god that is worshiped by only these Jews!"

The old man answered mildly, "But I have offered to teach the lad for very little, my lord, if you will but allow me one day in seven in which to rest."

"One day in seven," Cornelius sneered. "Six days for study, then a day in which he forgets all that he has learned in the six!"

"I have not found it so, my lord. I have proved to myself that with a day of rest I can do more work in six days than I formerly did in seven. I ask only that you give me a trial."

Madoc could see that Cornelius was frowning angrily. "That is hard to believe, but we shall see."

Madoc saw him glance at the bronze sundial that stood on a marble pedestal in the middle of the garden. Its shadow was turned slightly toward the east. "See, it is an hour past noon," he said to Orestes. "Come at this same hour every day. Your wages will be paid at the end of each week."

The old man started away, then turned, hesitating. "If you could pay me a day's wages in advance, my lord, I— There is no food in my house. I was about to sell my books, but they are very dear to me." His fingers tightened about the bundle of scrolls.

Cornelius answered with an exclamation of impatience. He tossed a silver coin. The Greek picked it up from the pavement at his feet. Then, with a quiet word of thanks, he went out through the narrow gate in the high stone wall that enclosed the garden.

Cornelius paced back and forth along the walk. Finally, he glanced up at Madoc, still waiting beside the pillar. "Well, well, why do you stand there? Are the letters in the hands of the ship's captain?"

"Yes, my lord."

"Then attend to my words. Every afternoon the Greek will come. He will teach you to read and write. At the end of the week, while he rests on his Jewish Sabbath, you will prepare me a copy of all that you have learned."

His sharp glance was like Gratus' bullwhip in its crackling threat. "You will do no loitering. Make no mistake about that."

"Yes, no, my lord."

Madoc went in search of Hannibal to tell him the news. He found him in an alcove that opened off the kitchen. The African was pushing a wooden handle that rolled one heavy stone over another on which it fitted, capwise. There was a hole in the top of the upper stone, and into this Hannibal poured wheat to be ground into flour. The African's dark body was thoroughly dusted, and his flour-whitened eyelashes gave him a ghostly look. Madoc watched for a moment as the ground wheat drifted down into a trough that went around the edge of the lower millstone. The noise made it impossible for him to be heard.

When Hannibal paused to pour more wheat into the mill,

Madoc spoke to him. "Why do you think a master would pay wages to someone to teach a slave to read and write?" he asked.

The African shook his flour-dusty head. With an anxious glance toward the kitchen he muttered, "Don't bother me, lad! Anna says if I don't get this flour ready by the time she needs it, she will lay more stripes across my lazy back. She doesn't like slaves to stand around. You better go and find out what she wants you to do."

Madoc chuckled at the thought of the tiny black-haired woman putting the lash to the powerful Hannibal. But he went back to the kitchen for orders.

Anna's sharp eyes, darting from head to toe, soon wiped all chuckling from his mind. "Your face is streaked with dust and your hair uncombed." She glanced at his belt. "Your girdle is carelessly tied, and there is a bulge in your tunic, as if you had something hidden."

She snatched at the knot, but he ducked away. His hands covered the bulge where he had tucked away a piece of bread, left over from his lunch.

Anna stared a moment into his rebellious blue eyes. They were on a level with her own. Suddenly her face softened.

"If it is a part of your lunch that you are saving, lad, you will find there is no need. Your master will give you food in plenty, so long as you remain an obedient servant."

She called to Reuben and spoke rapidly in her own tongue. Then to Madoc she said, "You are to go every morning to the

market with Reuben. You will watch and listen, so that in time
you can go alone."

Madoc was delighted. He would have gone back to the
grinding mill to tell Hannibal, but Anna sent him about his
business.

He paused in the doorway. Bread, it seemed, baked on the
open hearth in a Roman villa on the Judean coast, smelled
just as it did in a snug log house in the hills of Gaul. He closed
his eyes for a moment and pretended. It was not Anna but
his mother, tall and golden-haired, who was leaning over the
hearth to turn the loaves.

CHAPTER 6: THE SYRIAN PEDDLER

Madoc's days slipped into a busy pattern that left little time for remembering or for thoughts of revenge. Early every morning he went to the barracks, where he learned to polish and sharpen the swords and lances and battle-axes that the soldiers used. He learned to adjust a helmet and breastplate, even to cleanse and bind small wounds. Upon returning to the villa he went with Reuben to the market and watched as the little Jew bargained with the farmers. The talk was always in Aramaic, and as weeks passed, Madoc came to understand more and more of it. Before the coming of the barley harvest, he could venture into small conversations.

"Where did this fruit come from?" he asked one day of a girl who sat beside a basket of dried grapes.

The young woman glanced up to see if his ear bore the brand of a slave. Then she politely said, "From Hebron."

Madoc lifted a small cluster, plucked a grape, and tasted it. "What is the cost?"

"Two clusters for a penny."

Madoc shook his head. "That is too much."

The girl cried out that he knew nothing of the price of dried grapes. "They have come all the way over the mountains." She lifted two large bunches. "This many, with the cluster you hold in your hand for a penny."

Madoc insisted on four bunches. His voice grew louder as hers became shrill with excitement. Finally she gave up, muttering angrily against foreigners who came with the cruel Romans to rob her people.

Madoc could not understand all she said, but he knew that this noisy bargaining was part of the business of buying and selling. Now he dropped the four choicest bunches into his market basket. He looked up to see Reuben smiling in his wispy gray beard.

As he turned away from the fruit stall, Madoc noticed a dark-eyed man standing nearby. The stranger was wearing heavy gold earrings that flashed in the sun. Madoc had started to walk away with Reuben when suddenly the man called out a greeting in the Gallic tongue.

Madoc's stomach seemed to completely turn over. His heart pounded at the sound of the familiar words.

"May the Gods protect you," he burst into eager reply. "May you be warmed by the sunshine, and may you find success in all that you undertake! Who are you, and when have you come from my homeland?"

The man grinned and held up his hand to stop the flow of words. He answered in the tongue of the Romans. "I know only the greetings of your people. I am a peddler from Damascus.

Every year I visit the provinces of Gaul with my wares." He peered curiously into Madoc's face. "But you, lad, how came you to this faraway land?"

Eagerly Madoc poured out the story of his father's death, and his own capture, and even briefly the sorry tale of his mother. The peddler listened, but with obvious indifference when he learned that Madoc was merely a slave. Then, at word of his mother, the stranger's sharp eyes grew narrow.

Reuben, meanwhile, stood by. He was unable to understand the conversation, but he watched the peddler with worried eyes.

The Syrian peddler asked, "Are you sure that your mother is in Cremona at the weaving mill?"

Madoc could not be sure, but he said, "I heard the slave traders say that she was."

The peddler remarked, "There is a weaver named Julius in Cremona. I have often taken the wool of his weaving over the mountains into Gaul."

"If I could only have seen her," Madoc burst out. "If I could have given her just a word of hope—"

The Syrian was watching coldly. Madoc's voice became unmanageable, just as it had when he told his story to Cornelius. At sight of his twisting lip, a crafty look came into the peddler's eyes.

"I might be able to see your mother," he said, "when I go into Italy at the time of the early rains."

Madoc caught his breath. His face flushed with the shock
of delight. "You would—you could carry a message to my
mother?"

The peddler's lips drew in. "I doubt if I could speak to
your mother. Julius is a stern master. And with the noise of
the looms, it would not be possible to make her hear unless I
shouted. But perhaps, for a price, I might drop a letter into her
lap in passing."

A letter? Madoc's heart sank. He could not write a letter. But
he was learning! Already he could write a number of words.
Perhaps Orestes could teach him in time!

The man was speaking again. "I go now to Damascus. Upon
my return, I will look for you here."

He started away. Madoc came back to earth with a sickening
jolt. He ran after the peddler. He held out empty hands. "The
price!" he cried. "I am a slave! I could not pay!"

The Syrian glanced cautiously at the anxious Reuben. Then
he whispered, "Your master is a rich man. A penny here, a
penny there, perhaps from the marketing—"

Madoc shook his head.

"A pity," sneered the peddler, "that so small a thing as a
denarius or two should stand between you and a letter to your
mother!"

Madoc choked a little. "I—I can try, my lord. And, yes! I will
meet you here at the time of the rains."

The peddler was gone. Madoc, still confused, rejoined Reuben. Would his fellow slave report the matter to their master? Would he, Madoc, be compelled to tell Cornelius all that had happened? Would he be forbidden to see the peddler again?

There was plenty of time to think and plan. And I must pray to Mabon, he told himself, that these things may not come to pass. Secretly he vowed that he would meet the Syrian, even if it meant disobeying his master, and that somehow he would get the necessary money.

"Anna," he asked as soon as they reached home, "when is the time of the rains?"

She lifted the basket of fruit from his hands. "The early rains come in four months or a little more."

Madoc's mind was far from settled when in the afternoon his teacher came for the day's lessons.

Orestes greeted him as was his custom: "May the peace of God be with you, my son."

The lesson began with words written by Orestes on the wax tablet. They were words that Madoc must learn to read and write and spell. Today, however, his mind was not on his work. Could he, in four months' time, learn to write a letter?

"My lord," he burst out, "if I learn each day the words of the lesson, would you teach me also a few of my own choosing?"

Orestes lifted his brows in question. "What are the words you are eager to learn?"

"I should like to write my own name and the name of my mother. And then, perhaps, the word 'god.'"

"What do you know of God?" the Greek inquired.

"Only that there are many gods, and I have decided to find mine in Mabon, the sun-god of my people."

Orestes answered, almost in a whisper, "There is only one God over all the world, the moon, and the sun."

Suddenly he picked up the stylus and said, "Come now, let us get on with the lesson. 'Boy' is written so, and 'wolf' so. Now make the copy."

Madoc was not discouraged. Somehow he would manage to slip in the words he needed, along with the ones Orestes thought he should learn.

As he wrote, he pondered the strange thing that the Greek had said. "Only one God over all the world—"

Finally, he sat back with a sigh. "Sir," he inquired, "are there not many gods in your land, as in mine?"

"There are images of stone and marble and bronze," Orestes agreed. "But God is not in them. He is a living God, who cares for his people and hears their prayers. His words have been preserved for us in the holy writings."

Here indeed was a new thing! Madoc was amazed. "Tell me about these writings. Mabon the sun-god does not speak. Indeed, I am not sure that he hears me when I pray."

The Greek replied sternly, "It is the living God who has made the sun—and the moon and the stars as well. Every good gift is from him."

Madoc's mouth dropped open. Finally, he whispered, "Is a slave permitted to hear these holy writings?"

"No man is a slave in the sight of God," Orestes replied in a lowered tone. He glanced quickly toward the house, then went on, "Hear now a song of one of God's faithful followers. He was a king in this land many years ago."

Madoc laid down his stylus. He watched the face of the old man who repeated softly, "'The Lord is my shepherd, I shall not want...'"

Madoc had tended sheep on the hillsides of his homeland. He knew of the care that a good shepherd gives his sheep. He listened closely until Orestes concluded: "'Surely goodness and mercy shall follow me all the days of my life, and I shall dwell in the house of the Lord forever!'"

Madoc continued to stare. Was there a God who truly loved his people? Who watched over them as a shepherd guarded his sheep?

"Good teacher," he whispered, "since in the sight of your God I am not a slave, would it be permitted that I learn the words of that song?"

Neither Madoc nor Orestes knew that Cornelius had come out onto the porch and had stood behind a pillar listening to this strange interruption of the day's lessons. Therefore Madoc was startled and not a little frightened when, upon the last day of the week, his master looked up from inspecting Madoc's work.

"Is there not something more you have learned?" the centurion asked. "Have you not, of your own wish, memorized a song?"

Madoc met his master's stern gaze. "I have, my lord, but I know not if you wish to hear it."

"A slave is not called upon to make decisions for his master! What is it you have learned?"

"It—it concerns not the gods of Rome, my lord. Rather, it is in praise of the God that Orestes worships."

"I have heard of him," Cornelius answered, as if for a moment he had forgotten he was speaking to a slave, "and I would know more."

Then suddenly he thundered, "Give me the words of that song!"

Madoc began haltingly, then went on in greater confidence as he noticed that the centurion's eyes were closed.

When the song was finished, Cornelius still sat with closed eyes. "'Goodness and mercy,'" he repeated to himself. "I wish—I wish—"

Suddenly he leaped to his feet. "I know not what I wish! This God of the Jews—what has he to do with me?"

He turned to Madoc. "Away with you! Keep out of my sight until you are called!"

Madoc backed out of the room so hurriedly that he bumped into a door post. "I hope I have not angered him," he whispered to the little marble cherub in the pool. Suddenly he remembered the letter to his mother, and his heart turned sick with fear. He could not possibly write that letter until he had learned a great many more words. "I hope, I pray," he added earnestly, "that he may not send Orestes away!"

And yet he did not hate his master the more for his angry words. For some reason that Madoc could not explain, he was even a little sorry for the proud Roman.

CHAPTER 7: A STRANGE NEW WAY

On the following morning, Madoc awoke as usual before sunup. Quietly he slipped out of bed and tiptoed from the house to the barnyard, then over the gate to the hill path. As he climbed, the sky grew bright, the rounded hilltops gilt-edged. Then the sun appeared.

Madoc closed his eyes against its glare as he lifted his hands to pray, as on previous mornings: "O mighty Mabon, god of the day, giver of heat and light—"

He stopped. Was the sun anything more than a ball of fire? Orestes had a living God. A God that loved his people and heard them when they prayed.

Madoc lowered his hands and looked away. But how did one speak to this God of all the world? Orestes had not told him that.

He lifted his hands again, this time open-eyed, with his back to the sun. "'The Lord is my shepherd,'" he said aloud as sparrows began to twitter in every thornbush and tree, "'I shall not want.'"

When the song was finished, he raced back down the hill. He had not asked Orestes' God to punish Gratus, or avenge the cruelty of the guard on shipboard. He had not even asked that his teacher be not sent away! He had prayed to a God that promised "goodness and mercy," and he had clambered over the gate into the barnyard with a strange new feeling of satisfaction.

As he entered the courtyard, Madoc heard the noise of the grinding mill and Hannibal's voice. It was raised in song as gay and unimportant as the twittering of the field sparrows.

As Madoc poked his head in at the kitchen doorway, Anna caught him by the ear. "Bring me wood for the fire," she snapped. "The master will be calling for his breakfast before it is ready! Must you call his anger down upon all of us with your careless ways? Have you been out again, crowing with the cock?"

She loosed his ear for a quick smack to his grinning face, but Madoc darted away. He built a fire of brush and had the oven heated before she had finished kneading the bread.

Cornelius went into the city soon after breakfast. When he returned at midday, Madoc heard him stride through the great entrance hall to the library. Then came an impatient handclap.

"Bring me a stylus and tablet," the centurion snapped as Madoc hurried in.

Cornelius' heavy brows were drawn together until they nearly met above his narrow nose. Madoc backed away and waited just inside the doorway. Was his master still angry about the song Orestes had taught him? Or had Reuben finally told him about the Syrian peddler? His heart skipped a beat as he thought of that, although he realized it was unlikely, after so long a time. He jumped as Cornelius closed the wax tablet with a bang.

"I am called into the field," the centurion snapped. "You and Hannibal will go with the wagons. We travel far and fast. I have ordered donkeys for you to ride."

He handed the tablet to Madoc. "Take this to the barracks. Say it is a message from Cornelius the centurion. Go!"

As Madoc started away, Cornelius called him back. "When your teacher comes this afternoon, tell him that you will be away two, possibly three weeks. I will send for him when we return."

Madoc knew that the horsemen, as well as the foot soldiers, were housed at the barracks. They were long low buildings at the foot of the cliff on which the castle stood. As he raced through the city gates, he pressed the tablet to his chest and planned. It would never do to lose even two weeks' time from learning the words he needed for his mother's letter. He would take up the matter with Orestes. He laughed with relief when he remembered that his teacher was not to be dismissed because of the song!

When Madoc returned to the villa, he heard voices in the reception hall. He stopped at the doorway and looked in. A tall dark stranger stood beside the front door. His fringed silken headdress was bound around by a rope of camel's hair. His long striped mantle came almost to his feet. The stranger's name, Madoc learned, was Faduel. He was a desert tribesman, apparently of some importance, who was being hired to lead the Roman horsemen on a mission into the desert.

After final bargainings and instructions, the man backed through the doorway. The fringe of his headdress nearly swept the floor as he bowed himself out.

"Madoc," called the centurion, "Put the bar across the door. See that my breastplate is polished, my lance is cleaned and sharpened, everything in readiness as you have been instructed at the barracks. Reuben will help you. Remember, you must be ready at all hours of the day or night to carry out my orders. I shall expect instant obedience. See to it that you do not forget!"

"Yes, my lord."

The centurion's voice, Madoc decided, was as sharp as the two-edged sword he was about to polish. He was thankful to get away and report to Reuben.

They were still at work when the knocker on the garden gate announced the coming of Orestes. Madoc sighed as he ran to lift the iron bar that locked it. There had not even been time for lunch!

"Today," said Orestes, "you shall read your first story."

He drew from the front of his tunic a scroll of papyrus and handed it to Madoc. "I have saved it for a surprise."

"Why!" Madoc exclaimed as he unrolled the scroll. "Here are the words I have learned to read and to write! It is the story of two boys and a wolf!" He glanced on a little farther. "A wolf who mothered them!"

Orestes was smiling. "You will soon be able to read it all, my son. Never has a pupil learned so fast. See, it is the tale of Romulus and Remus, the two brothers who founded Rome."

Madoc read on with keen delight. He remembered the books on the shelves in the master's library—heavy scrolls of papyrus, a few of parchment. Each one had a tab hanging from the end of the roll on which was written the name of the book. Was it possible that someday he would be able to read, not only the names on the tabs, but the contents of the scrolls as well? It was a thrilling thought, as exciting as exploring an unknown land.

He toiled on with Romulus to build the walls of ancient Rome. After an hour's work, he looked up suddenly. "Sire, I have not yet told you the words of my master. He is taking me away for a time, and I may have no more lessons until we return. He bade me tell you that he will send for you then."

Madoc smiled directly into the eyes of his teacher. "Since nothing will be required of me by my master, could you not make for me, copies of certain words, that I may learn to write them while I am away?"

Orestes was pleased. "You are indeed eager to learn, my son! Take with you the scroll from which you have just read. On the back of it, I will make for you copies of the words you give me." He picked up his reed pen. "Now, the words."

Madoc repeated a list he had arranged in his mind. "I should like also," he concluded, "the name of the city and the land in which I am living, and the name of my master."

He watched, delighted, as Orestes wrote. It was good—
almost too good to be true! It made practically certain the
writing of the letter to his mother. All that remained now was
the problem of money to pay the peddler. He had no wish to
steal from his master. And there was nothing that he could sell
for a denarius. Nothing, that is, but the cloak that his mother
had made for him. Could he bring himself to part with it?

Orestes handed him the scroll. "While you are in camp, you
can practice by scratching the words on smooth stones or pieces
of broken pottery that you will find wherever you go. Then,
when you have learned them well, you may write them on the
scroll below the copies that I have set for you."

When he got up to leave, Orestes placed his hand on Madoc's
shoulder. "Every day I shall pray for you, my son, that you and
your master may return safely."

Madoc thanked him. Then he added, "How is it that you would
pray for a slave? And for a Roman who thinks nothing of your
God? Can it be that your God would care for him and for me?"

Orestes looked deep into Madoc's inquiring eyes. Then he
sat down again on the stone bench. "I know, lad, that you are
asking for the truth. And I must give it to you, even though it
bring down upon my head the anger of your master."

He spoke in a cautious whisper. Madoc listened, trying to fix
every word in his mind.

"Many hundreds of years ago, God chose the children of
a man named Abram to be his people until the time when

a Savior should come. This Savior, so said God's promise to Abram, would be a blessing to all the people of the earth."

He paused. "Do you understand, my son?"

"You mean, good teacher, that the Savior was promised to all people? To the Greeks and Romans—and the people of Gaul, even though they be slaves?"

"Even so. Not one was left out."

Madoc's breath came quickly as the learned man went on: "About fifty years ago the promised Savior came to this land of Judea. His name was Jesus. He taught a new way—a good way of living. A way of forgiveness to all who have wronged us. Remember, my son, that I, too, have been a slave to the Romans. I shall pray that you and your master may return safely—because I am a follower of the new Way."

Madoc walked to the gate with Orestes. He lowered the iron bar into its slot without knowing what he did. The strange words rang in his ears as he turned back toward the house. He climbed the two steps to the porch. Forgiveness for Gratus? For the judge who had sent his mother into slavery? For the man whose slave he was?

A sharp handclap recalled him. He went quickly to the upper room where he slept beside his master. His low couch had been pulled from under Cornelius' bed. The centurion was looking with scorn at the plaid cloak, soiled and worn, that Madoc had hidden under his pallet.

Cornelius picked it up on the point of his sword and held it at arm's length. "Take it away!" he ordered. "Take it to the kitchen and put it into the fire. No servant of mine shall be seen in such a garment."

"Oh, master," Madoc cried out, "I need not wear it, but is all that I have from—"

"Silence!" thundered the centurion. "Do as I tell you without delay!"

Madoc snatched the cloak from the sword's point. He clasped it close to his body. He stumbled, because he could not see. He buried his lips deep in the folds of his treasure and cried, "No, no! I cannot! It is too much! I will not!"

He had reached the courtyard. Hannibal looked up from his hedge clipping. "Wait, lad, where do you go in such haste? Don't tell me that you are trying again to run away!"

Madoc stopped in his headlong flight. Where was he going? Hannibal was right. There was no place where he could flee from his master—no place where he could hide the cloak.

Slowly he walked back until he stood before his fellow slave. He pushed the cloak into the hands of the astonished African.

"Cast it—into the fire! The master commands it!"

He turned his back. He knew that Hannibal, muttering deep in his throat, had started slowly toward the kitchen. Madoc did not look around. The words of Orestes came back to mock him. Kindness? Forgiveness? Their meaning was drowned in the waves of hatred that swept over him like a storm.

When, an hour later, the centurion tossed him a discarded cloak of his own, Madoc took it without a word. He folded it and laid it on his bed. Then he went to the oven and peered inside. A scrap of the cloak was still smoldering near the door. He snatched it out, smothered the sparks between his fingers, and took it to the room where he had first slept. There he hid it under Hannibal's pallet of straw.

CHAPTER 8: THE GOATHERD

Early the next morning, Madoc and Hannibal went to the stables. There they were to be provided with donkeys for the journey.

Madoc spoke to a soldier who was shouting orders. "We are the servants of Cornelius," he began. "Our master has told us—"

"Your beasts are there, tied to a post," the man interrupted.

Madoc looked. Two rough-haired little animals were standing with lowered heads. Long ears flapped lazily to keep the flies away. Madoc laid a hand on the thick, upstanding mane of a donkey. There was neither saddle nor bridle—only a saddle cloth and the hempen rope by which the beast was tied.

"Hannibal," he confessed, "I have never ridden one of these creatures. Do you think it will obey my commands?"

The African was standing with both hands resting on the slender back of the other donkey. He shook his head. "Nor have I. Feel most ashamed to. I so big and he so little."

Nearby stood a number of horse-drawn wagons. They were being loaded for the journey with long, iron-pointed lances and wooden, leather-covered shields. On other wagons Madoc saw tents and crates of live chickens and hand mills in which the soldiers would grind their own wheat from day to day.

Finally the order was given to move. The teamsters shouted, and the wagons pulled out of the stable yard. Hannibal boosted Madoc to an uneasy seat on his donkey. Then he gave his own animal a shove and a hearty smack of his broad palm. As the donkey started, he ran alongside and jumped on.

Madoc, his heart in his mouth, shouted, "Go!"

The donkey flicked a sand fly from its ear and lowered its head in complete unconcern. The wagons were drawing away. "Hannibal," Madoc shouted, "what does one do now?"

A stableman came up behind. He belabored the little animal with a stick. Without any warning, the beast humped its back into an up-curving half moon. Madoc promptly slipped off over its tail. Red-faced, he got to his feet. The donkey was now racing madly after the others, its lead rope dangling.

"Here," said the stableman, "take this club. The creature is clever as well as lazy. It has learned already that you do not know how to handle it. Now, after them!"

Madoc soon overtook the donkey and mounted again. The animal started off at once into a clattery trot that almost jarred Madoc loose again. He wrapped his legs about the animal's body and clung to the thick mane with both hands.

There was no sign of Cornelius or his soldiers as the caravan moved southward along a stone-paved highway. When they were well away from the stables, Madoc discovered that his donkey needed neither guiding nor urging. The little beast appeared to have no interest in life except to stay with the caravan.

They traveled for a short distance southward along the shore of the sea. On their right were big yellow sand dunes and smaller hillocks of broken shells brought in by the waves. Looking inland, Madoc could see nothing but scrubby little pine trees, like tattered beggars, their garments worried by the wind.

Soon the road turned away from the sea, to avoid even higher sand dunes that blocked the way. It led through a beautiful grassy plain. Everywhere flocks were feeding, each with its own watchful shepherd close by.

Camp was pitched early, on the outskirts of a small walled town that was built on a ridge overlooking the sea. Madoc helped Hannibal raise the tents and bring water from the town well. Then he watched with interest as flour was ground in the small hand mills, shaped into flat loaves, and baked over campfires by the soldiers. Cornelius and Faduel did not ride into camp until dark. The next morning they, with the horsemen, were up with the sun. Madoc watched as they rode away, separating to range over the eastern plains.

Now the highway turned eastward, and the caravan made its slow way toward the hill country. Madoc got off often to walk. The rough hair of his donkey had made his legs sore, and his back and neck were strained by the constant motion of the beast.

As they came near the hills, Madoc saw that the slopes were covered with orchards and vineyards and gardens, all in the beauty of full leaf.

Late in the afternoon the wagons drew up in the shade of a sycamore grove, near the ruined gates of a town. The work of making camp began at once.

The day was hot, and Madoc took off his tunic. Dressed only in a loincloth, he helped Hannibal unload and raise the master's tent. Then he took a water jar and went to bring water from a brook that made its way down through the broken walls of the town.

As he came near the stream, Madoc noticed a small flock of goats on the opposite bank. The goatherd was nowhere to be seen. Madoc lay down on his stomach and drank deeply, then splashed the cool water over his face and body.

As he leaned over to fill the earthen jar, he heard a voice. It came from behind an oak tree near which the goats were nipping twigs from the brush.

"Ho, pale skin, why do you not cover your white face when you do the work of a woman?"

Madoc filled his jar, set it down, then stood up. "Come out," he shouted in reply, "Come closer and judge if I fight like a woman!"

There was no further sound from behind the tree. Madoc waited and watched. Then he picked up his jar and set it on his shoulder. Slowly he turned his back to the oak tree and started up the slope toward the camp.

Suddenly came the swish of a stone and a stabbing pain between his shoulder blades. He stumbled and pitched forward onto his face. The water jar slid from his numbed arms and crashed into a hundred pieces on the rocks. Blood was running from his bruised nose when he got to his feet. He staggered dizzily for a moment, then turned.

A boy of his own age was dancing up and down on the opposite bank of the stream. Madoc heard him shout, "Woman! White skin! Ho, ho, ho!"

Madoc wiped the blood from his face with the back of his hand. His mind cleared. With the yell of a Gallic warrior, he plunged back down the slope and into the water.

"Wait, lad, wait!" shouted a voice from the direction of the town. Madoc scarcely heard. The goats scattered in panic as he splashed across the stream, up the opposite bank, and after his tormentor.

There was a moment of wild delight as Madoc brought the goatherd crashing to the ground on his face. Again and again he banged his fist into the fallen boy's back, then rubbed his face into the sand.

Suddenly Madoc was lifted bodily into the air and set upon his feet. The other boy scrambled up to face him.

There was a long pause. Panting, the two boys glared into each other's bloody face, then up at the man who had stepped between them.

"Aaron!" It was the voice of the man who had called upon Madoc to wait. "Aaron, my son, how has this come about? Are you not a follower of the Way?"

He laid a hand on the goatherd's shoulder. "Tell me, did the Master promise a blessing upon the makers of war?"

Aaron wiped the sand from his nose and mouth. He mumbled without looking up, "No, my lord."

"What then?"

The goatherd cast a sullen look at Madoc, then hung his head again. "He—he promised blessing—to the makers of peace."

Madoc stared first at Aaron, then at the man whose hand still rested on the goatherd's shoulder. He noticed that the stranger's beard was white and that his shoulders stooped like those of Orestes. Though his eyes were kind, his next question was spoken sternly.

"And what did he say about hating our enemies?"

The goatherd's reply could scarcely be heard. "Not—not to hate, but to love them!"

Madoc listened in amazement. Had he heard right? Was it not the part of a brave man to fight? To do his enemy as much hurt as possible?

The man's quiet voice went on, still speaking to Aaron. "And if you have wronged another, even though he be of lighter skin and from a far country, what would the Master have you do?"

Aaron burst out, "But, good teacher, the boy comes from the camp of the hated Romans! He is one of them!"

The man insisted, "Even though he be one of them, what would the Master have you do?"

Now at last Aaron looked up. His dark eyes were no longer angry. "Sir, I know not. What would the Master have me do?"

The man took Madoc's arm and turned him about. "See the great pain you have caused! The deep wound and the blood!"

Madoc glanced uneasily over his shoulder as Aaron touched his back. There followed another long pause. At last the goatherd muttered, "I ask the stranger to forgive. And to pay for the wrong, I give him the slingshot with which I bruised him."

"Well spoken, my pupil!" cried the man. He turned to Madoc as Aaron held out his peace offering.

"You, lad, can you find it in your heart to forgive?"

Madoc stared in unbelief. Perhaps he had misunderstood. And yet, there was the slingshot dangling from the boy's outstretched fingers. Suddenly it reminded him of the centurion, holding out a cloak that dangled from the point of a sword.

He snatched Aaron's gift and turned to run away. His face was twisted with anger. "Forgive?" he shouted. "I know not the meaning of the word!"

He reached camp just as Cornelius, at the head of twenty horsemen, came riding into view. Madoc ducked out of sight among the tents, then looked back. Madoc knew that a centurion was a captain of foot soldiers. He also knew that these soldiers could, if necessary, fight on horseback. Now he saw that his master was easily the best rider of them all.

Hannibal ran to catch the horse's bridle as Cornelius dismounted. Madoc hastily put on his tunic and thrust the slingshot into the front of it. He was waiting beside the tent door as his master strode in.

The centurion was in a dark mood. "Take my helmet; my breastplate. Bring water in a basin."

Madoc took the heavy shield and helmet. He gritted his teeth against the pain in his back. He unbuckled the sheath in which the centurion carried his long sword, then backed out hurriedly with his clanking burden.

When Madoc returned with water and towels, Cornelius was grumbling about the heat, the dust, the fact that his tent was poorly shaded. "Always at harvest time," he growled to himself. "I must go out into the desert to chase those thieving Arabs back into the southland! A curse upon them all!"

Madoc knelt to remove his master's shoes, then poured water on his hands and feet. As he bent over with the towel to dry Cornelius' feet, suddenly the grumbling ceased.

"What has happened to you?" the centurion asked sharply. "Whence comes the blood that is soaking through your tunic? And how has your face been bruised?"

Madoc tried to keep his face turned away as he mumbled, "I went to bring water. A boy at the brook did cast a stone at me with his slingshot and I fell on my face."

"And you?" Cornelius snapped when he had waited in vain for Madoc to say more. "Did you repay him in his own coin?"

"Yes," Madoc admitted. "I beat him and rubbed his face in the sand."

Another pause. Finally the centurion shouted, "Son of a barbarian, how is it that you answer me in only as many words as pleases you? Tell me the meaning of all this! How did it come to pass?"

Madoc stood up. With eyes still turned away, he told the story briefly. "And at the last," he concluded, lifting his head, "the gray-bearded teacher asked me to forgive, but—" the slave boy was remembering the cloak as he met his master's eyes, "I told the man I knew not the meaning of the word."

Madoc, his back still throbbing with pain, waited to be dismissed.

At last Cornelius muttered to himself, "A—blessing upon the makers of peace! A command to forgive—to love one's enemies!"

He lifted frowning eyes to meet those of his waiting servant. Suddenly he shouted, "'Tis enough to turn the world upside down! Away with you! 'Tis not necessary that you know the meaning of the word!"

Madoc darted from the tent.

Nothing more was said. When his work was finished, Madoc lay down to sleep at the feet of his snoring master. He marveled as he remembered the change that had come over the goatherd when reminded of a Master who commanded his followers to love and forgive. But how was it possible to forgive the Romans who had killed his father and enslaved his mother? Surely this Master had never known such hateful men, or he would have known it was not possible!

Unable to sleep for the pain in his back, Madoc sat up on his straw pallet. He recalled the promised prayers of Orestes. Was it possible that Aaron's Master and Savior of whom Orestes had told him were one and the same? He lay down on his stomach and tried to sleep again. But something was hurting in his chest. It was almost as bad as the pain in his back. Madoc was remembering his own shouted reply when the goatherd's teacher had asked him to forgive.

CHAPTER 9: IN CAMP

Long before dawn Madoc was wakened from a restless sleep. He gathered fuel for the ovens, carried water from the brook, and went to get the donkeys that were pastured a short distance from the tents. Then he brought freshly baked bread and cheese and wine, and served his master's breakfast in the cool shade of the sycamores.

Cornelius stared again at Madoc's bruised and swollen face. "Were the goatherd's wounds as bad as yours?"

"No, my lord."

"Then why did you not deal him a final blow when he came near to hand you his worthless gift?"

Madoc replied, "I no longer hated him."

Cornelius glowered. "You had no wish to take full revenge for a wound as bad as that on your back? For a face as battered as yours? Perhaps you were afraid?"

Madoc flushed. "There was a strange new feeling, my lord. I know it was not fear. But the new feeling did battle with the anger that had made me strike him."

He said no more. Cornelius growled to himself, "I cannot but wonder about a man who would teach this strange new way of living. It must be that he is crazy!"

Breakfast was soon finished, and Madoc heard Cornelius tell the leader of the caravan they would make their next stop at Joppa. Before the wagons were loaded, the horsemen rode away, with Cornelius and the guide Faduel at their head. They would range over the countryside in search of the bandits from the south.

Madoc drove his donkey up beside Hannibal's. He looked down upon the rolling plains. They were dotted with villages, which were surrounded by olive and fig orchards, and fields of wheat, yellow and ready to harvest.

Hannibal had said nothing about Madoc's skinned face and bloodstained garment. Now he remarked, "You must have been fighting, lad, or else the master got pretty angry with you."

Madoc was thinking. "I did fight with a goatherd from the town."

Hannibal shook his head in sympathy or disapproval, Madoc did not know which.

Suddenly Madoc asked, "Did you ever feel like killing somebody because he had wronged you?"

Hannibal rubbed the back of his neck. "Can't remember anything like that."

"But don't you hate the men who dragged you from your home? And the man who owns you now?"

The African's white teeth gleamed in the sunlight. He shook his head. "The master gives me a warm cloak to wrap me in when the nights are cold, and a beautiful yellow loin cloth, and ivory earrings. Should I hate him for that? Your talk mixes me up."

Madoc was becoming a bit confused himself. "But if the Romans had chained your mother to a loom and wouldn't let you see her, wouldn't even listen when you tried to ask—"

Hannibal had stopped his donkey. He was peering into the bushes that lined the roadside. "Come, lad, look at these birds' nests, stuffed in close together like a honeycomb! How do you suppose those mother birds ever find the right mouths to feed?" He shook his dark head and grinned. "Must be the gods made them wiser than us!"

The gods? Suddenly Madoc remembered. He had offered no prayer to Mabon since Orestes had told him about a living God!

Some time after noon, the caravan made its way through the gardens outside of Joppa. Tall palm trees waved in the breeze that came from the sea. All about were white stone houses, surrounded by beautiful irrigated gardens. Madoc heard for the first time the creak of water wheels where patient donkeys walked round and round to raise the water that kept the gardens green.

They stopped in the shade of the city's thick stone wall. Madoc was glad to rest and eat a lunch of bread and dried olives. Soon Cornelius and his horsemen appeared.

"Wash your face and smooth your hair," the centurion commanded Madoc as he sat down to eat. "We are going into the town."

Madoc ran to get water from a goatskin that hung at the back of a supply wagon. He cleaned his swollen face gingerly, then returned to walk behind the centurion through the gate and into the city.

"Where is the shop of one Simon the tanner?" Cornelius asked the question of a man who carried on his head a tray of fruits and small cakes.

The man pointed the way. Then he turned back to shout at the birds who hovered overhead, waiting for a chance to snatch a bit of food from his tray.

They entered a narrow cobblestoned street. Madoc looked with interest into the little sidewalk shops. He saw a jeweler, his dusky cheekbones red with the heat as he leaned over a pot of melted silver beneath which burned a fire of charcoal. In the street of bakers, he sniffed the delicious odor of baking bread and honey-sweetened cakes that were piled on trays or in wicker baskets.

"Master," he ventured, "I fear you have crossed the street of leather workers. 'Tis just there, behind us."

Cornelius stopped and looked around. "Eh? I did not notice." He cast a sharp glance into Madoc's upturned face. As he started back, he muttered unhappily, "Why must I go on thinking about a stupid goatherd and his teacher, who follow after a crazy dream?"

Madoc faced about. He stared at the back of his master's proud head, as if for the first time.

He followed as Cornelius turned in at the shop, larger than those about it. Inside it was dimly lighted and cool, and smelled pleasantly of leather. From the room at the rear of the shop came the cheerful voices of men at work.

An attendant in a short gray tunic came to greet them. Cornelius did not wait for him to speak. "I would see Simon the tanner," he said in the commanding manner that was the way of the Roman.

The attendant bowed and turned to fetch his master.

Madoc studied the merchant as he came toward them from the workshop. The elderly man walked slowly. His long garment of richly colored wool flowed in a smooth, rippling motion about his ankles. His sandals of red leather were soft and studded with jewels. He bowed, then waited for Cornelius to speak.

"I have heard of the beauty of the leather you make," the centurion began.

Simon bowed again, without smiling.

"Show me shoes and bridles and belts."

The merchant clapped his hands. Cornelius was invited to be seated while the articles were brought. Madoc stood close by as his master selected a pair of shoes with straps that crossed about his ankles, and a tiny pair of red sandals, made of softest leather. Suitable, Madoc decided, for a little girl. The centurion chose also a bridle and, finally, a girdle with a money pouch stitched to its inner side.

Simon, though he stood by and watched, took no part in the conversation. The money was paid to his attendant, and the tanner bowed again as Cornelius left the shop. Madoc, carrying the bundle of leather goods, followed close behind.

Before they reached the first corner, Madoc heard the sound of hurrying footsteps behind them.

"My lord!" called a voice. And then again, "My lord, the centurion!"

Madoc glanced back. "Master, Simon the tanner is calling you."

Cornelius stopped, frowning a little.

"Sir," said the tanner as he came near, "I ask your pardon. But I find that my servant, though without intent, charged you more than the rightful price. Take, please, the money that is yours!"

Cornelius stared. He held out his hand as if he knew not why. Then he looked down at the coins that Simon had dropped into it. "But—I do not understand! You—a Jew—would not take from a Roman all that you can?"

Simon bowed. "In former times, I did consider it no sin to take what I could from the oppressors of my people. We Jews considered that the wealth of our country rightfully belonged to us. But now—"

Cornelius snapped impatiently. "But now, what?"

"Now," Simon answered quietly, "I have come to know the Master. I am a follower of the Way."

He turned and walked back to his shop. Madoc stared after him. His gently billowing mantle was like rippling gold in the sunlight. Then Madoc glanced up into the face of his master. It was confused and unhappy.

Cornelius started on again, walking slowly. His head was bowed in thought. Madoc, too, was thinking. Why, it had almost seemed as if Simon the Jew wished his enemy well!

They came near the city gate. "Figs, dates, honey in the comb!" shouted the man with the tray on his head.

Cornelius beckoned to the seller of sweetmeats. He bought a cake of pressed dates, then turned and tossed it to the boy at his heels.

Taken by surprise, Madoc reached out to catch the dates. His bundle fell from his arms. As he stooped in, trembling, to snatch it from the dusty street, suddenly he cried out.

"Well," snapped Cornelius, "what is it with you?"

Madoc could feel the blood oozing down his back again. "The—the small wound between my shoulders, my lord. I think it has broken open anew. It—is nothing."

Cornelius said no more. They walked on to the resting place of the caravan outside the city walls. Soldiers and servants were lying in the shade. At a few short commands from the

centurion, the horsemen leaped to their mounts, the drivers to
their wagons. The caravan started without delay.

Madoc shared his sweets with Hannibal. The African was
now completely contented with life, except for one thing—the
size of his donkey.

"Can't understand how he keeps up with the wagons,"
Hannibal mumbled, his mouth full of sun-sweetened dates.
"Almost seems I should get off and carry him awhile."

Madoc did not answer. He was watching a woman who was
weaving tent cloth from the coarse black hair of goats. The warp
was stretched between two parallel sticks that were held to the
ground by heavy stones. The woman knelt with her back to the
highway. She leaned forward as she wove the thick yarn back
and forth over and under the strands that ran from stick to
stick. This was very different, Madoc thought, from the sturdy
oak loom in his mother's home.

"Hannibal," he called, "wait a moment and watch the
weaving! I have never seen the likes of it before."

The woman looked around angrily as she pushed the cross
threads down with a big wooden comb. "Begone with you!" she
shouted, and she shook the comb at them, club-wise. "Go your
way, sons of unbelievers!"

Madoc urged his donkey into a trot. It made his back throb
hotly. Not all the people of this land, he decided, had heard
about the new way of living.

Madoc noticed that Cornelius had kept close to the caravan, while his men rode over the rolling hills to their left.

Late in the afternoon Madoc saw a group of peasants hurrying toward them. They shouted to the centurion and poured out a torrent of wailings.

"Arabs!" was the cry. "Arabs have come from the desert!"

Madoc, eager to hear, hurried his donkey on past the wagons. The villagers were crying with as much breath as they could give to it.

"They have stolen our wheat, even from the field!" wailed their leader, an old man in a ragged gray mantle. "They have taken our cattle and scattered our sheep!"

Cornelius shouted to his scouting soldiers, then turned to the peasants.

"How long ago?" he asked. "In what direction did the Arabs leave?"

When the conversation was ended, the centurion called, "Madoc, bring me my shield and lance and a quiver of darts from the wagon."

The horsemen, led by Cornelius, soon disappeared among the sand dunes to the south. Madoc watched, then looked after the villagers as they, too, hurried away.

Camp was soon made. Madoc found a tree that spread all its branches eastward. It made him think of a woman turning her back to the sea wind, her garments blowing out before her.

There, with Hannibal's help, he raised Cornelius' tent.

The horsemen returned soon after dark. Grumbling, Cornelius ate his supper by the light of a torch. Darkness had kept them from overtaking the desert thieves.

He soon lay down to sleep. Madoc, at the foot of his master's bed, found it impossible to rest. His back still throbbed painfully, for the open wound was stiff with blood. Finally he sat up with a tired sigh.

"Why do you not lie still?" Cornelius asked sharply.

Madoc jumped. He had thought the centurion was asleep. "The pain in my back, my lord. It will not let me sleep."

Cornelius also sat up, yawning noisily. "Bring me a cruse of oil, a basin of water, and a napkin."

Madoc found in the cook tent a gourd bottle filled with olive oil, a large earthen jar of water, and linen cloths. He gathered them up and returned.

"Lie down on your face," ordered the centurion. "I am going to cleanse and anoint your wound."

CHAPTER 10: WITH A CARAVAN

Madoc awoke the next morning with a start. He had overslept! Cornelius' bed was empty! Terrified, he leaped from his mat. Why had he not been called to wait upon his master? He ran to the door of the tent. The horsemen had gone. It was the noise of breaking camp that had wakened him.

The morning was still cool as the caravan got underway. Madoc pulled his short tunic about him. He had never used the cloak that Cornelius had given him except to throw it over his bed at night.

They were still traveling southward. Madoc's eyes searched the plains for a glimpse of the soldiers. Would he be punished for sleeping late? Why had his master not called him? Somehow the touch of Cornelius' hands on his back the night before was hard to forget. He was sorry he had not wakened in time to bring the centurion his breakfast.

Late in the afternoon the horsemen were sighted. They were coming slowly across the desert toward the highway. Madoc looked for Cornelius' crested helmet.

Hannibal came near to watch with him. "See, lad, the master's horse is limping. A hurt in his shoulder."

No doubt a sword thrust, aimed at the rider, thought Madoc. He shivered a little.

"Hannibal!" Cornelius shouted when the horsemen were a short distance away.

The African ran forward to catch the horse's reins. Madoc was close behind. As he dismounted, the centurion pointed to the horse's wounded shoulder, from which blood had dripped to the knee. "Cleanse it with oil," he said, "and cover it with cedar tar. In the morning, bring me a fresh horse."

They had reached the outskirts of Gaza, a town by the sea. This was on the very edge of the great desert that was the home of the Arabs. Now Faduel directed the caravan to a camping place in a grove of ripening figs. Tents were quickly raised and supper prepared. Cornelius ate by the light of a small bronze lamp, then lay back on his couch to rest. He had spoken no word to Madoc, who had foreseen every possible wish of his master. Now Madoc gathered up his armor and sat down near the doorway to clean and polish it.

Almost at once the sound of hurrying footsteps caused him to look up from his task. It was the owner of the grove. He came, wringing his hands, and bowed before Cornelius. "Your horses and donkeys!" he wailed. "They eat the bark of my trees. And your servants eat the figs. I pray you, my lord, leave me in peace!"

The centurion, red-eyed and weary, glared at him. "Begone with you and your complaints! Have we not chased the thieving

Arabs out of your land? Is the fruit of your trees too good for the soldiers of Rome?"

The man folded his hands and bowed even more humbly. "But, my lord, I will bring chopped straw for the animals if you will but have your servants take them away from this grove."

Cornelius sat up on his couch. He lifted a clenched fist. "Take yourself away and leave me in peace!"

The man backed out of the tent, his gray beard resting on his chest.

Cornelius shot a quick glance at the watching Madoc. He dropped back on his pillow. "These peasants," he muttered. "They forget themselves."

Madoc noticed, however, that his master's eyes remained open. Glancing up from his work, he followed the centurion's frowning gaze. Cornelius was staring at the little red shoes that he had bought from Simon the tanner. His face was far from peaceful. He sighed impatiently and pounded his pillow with a clenched fist.

Madoc went on with his work. He listened for a time to the restless turnings, then he whispered, "Good master, if it would help you sleep better, Hannibal and I could tether the horses and donkeys outside the grove."

"See to it at once!" snapped the centurion. As Madoc hurried out into the darkness, Cornelius shouted after him, "And in the morning, tell the overseer to pay for all the figs our men have eaten!"

On the following day there was a hurried push directly eastward across the desert. The soldiers kept close to the caravan. Once Madoc caught a glimpse of the bandits, their gaily colored mantles blowing in the wind as they fled before the Roman horsemen.

They passed thorn-walled villages lying brown and sun-baked on the rocky plain. The wheat had been cut, and the little that had not been stolen was gathered into stacks on high threshing floors. Madoc watched as small red oxen walked round and round to tread the grain from the straw.

Late in the afternoon the horsemen disappeared. The caravan pushed on to a town called Hebron. Camp was made on a flat-topped hill overlooking the desert to the south.

Sometime in the night Cornelius came in. Madoc trembled with the shock of being suddenly wakened. He brought bread and wine to his weary master.

As Madoc lay down again to rest, suddenly the quiet of midnight was broken by a hideous screeching. "Master!" he cried, leaping from his bed. "What is that?"

"Lie down!" growled the sleepy centurion. "A hyena, hunting for his supper. He will not come into camp. He is a coward."

Next morning Madoc got up early. He looked out across the low hills and great barren plain to the south. It was strewn with rocks and scrubby thornbushes. In the dry river beds he could see a few small trees and a bit of green.

The rounded hills to the north were covered with olive groves. The hillside gardens were terraced and planted with gnarled grapevines that looked as old as the hills themselves.

Between the town and the hill on which Madoc stood was a village pool. He saw an old man in a long brown mantle waiting beside it. Soon a woman came from the town. She dipped her water jar into the pool, lifted it to the stone curb, and held it tilted for the old man to drink. That brought Madoc's mind to Aaron's taunt about the work of a woman.

Madoc turned again to look at the desert. He did not care to think about the goatherd.

"Madoc!" came a gruff call from within the tent.

Cornelius was preparing to leave again. Madoc brought water and breakfast, then stood beside the couch while the centurion ate hurriedly.

At the sound of crunching gravel they both turned. A group of men from the town came to stand in the doorway of the tent. The oldest among them stepped forward. "Peace be with you," he said.

"And to you," Cornelius replied in the language of the Jews. "What is the reason for your coming here?"

Their complaint was the same as that of the peasants along the way. Their grain had been stolen, their cattle driven off or killed.

Said the leader of the group, "They are the sons of Ishmael, these robbers! God said of him that his hand should be against every man—and so it has come to pass!"

Cornelius studied the man's angry face. He took a drink from his silver cup before he spoke. "To whom did your God speak this prophecy?"

"To Abraham, who was father both to us and to the Ishmaelites, who are now called Arabs."

"Very interesting," Cornelius remarked, as if he were not, in fact, interested at all. "And how does one call this God of yours?"

A younger man answered boldly, "He is Jehovah—and there is no other god."

Madoc watched and listened. Cornelius broke a small loaf into bits and dipped a piece into a pot of honey while the elder Jew tugged impatiently at his gray beard. Madoc was very sure that his master was more interested in this Jehovah than in the men's complaints. His next question startled even his servant.

"And this teacher of whom I have heard—who leads his followers in a new way of living—how does one call him?"

The villagers looked at one another in quick dismay. The face of the younger man lighted up. But before he could speak, their leader answered with a tight smile, "He—is of no concern to a Roman, my lord. Let us rather show you at once the direction in which the thieving Arabs have fled. Perhaps my lord can overtake them, and so return to us at least a part of our cattle."

The centurion's face grew suddenly red, and Madoc hastened to refill his master's cup. His hand was pushed aside and the wine was spilled. Cornelius leaped to his feet, but he did not speak again to the villagers.

"Call Faduel," he said to Madoc.

It was Faduel to whom the townsmen gave directions, after backing from the tent in uncertain confusion.

As he helped with his master's armor, Madoc heard their leader say, "Follow the course of the river that leads toward the south and west. At Beersheba, a place of two wells, you will find an encampment of shepherds. They are honest men and will direct you further."

In a few minutes the horsemen were ready to ride away.

"Do not leave the camp," Cornelius commanded Madoc as they started away. "Except to water the donkeys, go neither to the town nor to the desert. And no loitering at the pool."

Madoc could not imagine that he would care to leave the camp, for his mind was busy with plans. They concerned the scroll that Orestes had given him. Before the horsemen were out of sight among the rolling hills, he was collecting pieces of broken pottery on which to write the words he needed for the letter to his mother. He took the scroll from his knapsack and sat down to work in the shade of his master's tent.

Hannibal came to watch. He shook his head. "What you make, lad, with all those lines and curves? A charm to keep away the evil spirits of this wild land?"

Madoc shook his head and grinned. "A charm for my mother," he confided. "Something to give her hope. When one is chained, one must have hope, or else—"

The hours passed quickly. So did the days. Once his master had left in the early morning, there was little work for Madoc. He found that he was doing even better with his studies than if he had stayed at home with his teacher. Best of all, he told himself, I may learn only the words I need for the letter.

Each day, in the heat of noon, he took his donkey and Hannibal's to the pool. He chose that hour because no one was ever about to see him doing "the work of a woman."

It was on the fourth day at camp that Hannibal shouted to him from the doorway of the cook tent. "Sun is shining in your eyes, lad," he called. "Better move round to where the shade is."

Madoc grinned and rubbed his eyes. "Better still that I water the donkeys before the women start to come from the town."

He went to untie the animals. "They get pretty coltish, being tied so long," Hannibal called.

Madoc agreed as he started along the path that zigzagged down the hillside. He ran behind the two donkeys, sliding and stumbling, until the ropes jerked from his hands.

"Stubborn little beasts," he muttered, "may you die of thirst!"

There was little chance of that. Already they knew their way to the pool as well as he. They were waiting beside it when he arrived.

Madoc had just emptied his leather bucket into the trough for the last time when he lifted his head to listen. From the highway to the north came the song of a caravan leader, the jingle of bells, and the ill-natured growling of camels.

Madoc ran to pick up the ropes of the donkeys. They lifted dripping muzzles to follow him. When they were partway up the hill path, Madoc stopped to look back at the caravan. The camels were heavily loaded. The men, like the Syrian peddler at Caesarea wore gaily colored mantles with gold rings in their ears. The leader rode on a beautiful black mare beside his camels.

Madoc remembered that his master had told him not to loiter. But what harm could come from watching? He had never seen so large a caravan. Apparently its leaders were in a hurry to cross the desert, for they had not stopped at the pool.

He mounted his own donkey and sat at ease to watch. The swaying camels fascinated him. And the proud figure of the hawk-faced leader caused Madoc to straighten his own back.

He did not notice that the donkeys had pricked up their ears as the tinkling bronze bells drew nearer, then passed by on the highway close below them.

Suddenly, as if at a given signal, both animals whirled, pivoting on the narrow path. Madoc was almost thrown to the ground. He caught the short upstanding mane of his donkey with both hands. His guiding stick fell. Down the hill they went in a shower of dust and flying hoofs!

Madoc yelled at them, "Have you lost your senses?"

The animals ran on until they were close at the heels of the last camel in the caravan. As their wild pace slowed to a walk, Madoc jumped off. He tugged with all his weight on the hempen ropes, but the donkeys kept their steady gait.

Now they were turning westward, on the road by which Madoc had come from Gaza only a few days before.

He jumped on his donkey again. When we pass a bush or a tree, he decided, I will tie the beasts until the camels are out of sight. Then they will turn and go back willingly.

On they went. The sun slanted into Madoc's hot, red face. He was growing uneasy. His master was going to be angry because he had loitered. And what would he say when he learned that his servant had ridden with a caravan out into the desert?

Then suddenly, without any wish of his own, it came! The blinding, dizzying thought that here was the chance for which he had waited!

Madoc swayed. His heart pounded up against his throat. A jumble of misty thoughts and plans began to take shape in his brain. No one, not even Hannibal, had seen him go. Cornelius, as always, would be late in getting back to camp—much too late to start searching for a lost slave. Besides, he would not have the slightest suspicion that his servant had run away! Rather, he would decide that the Arabs had taken him—perhaps in revenge.

Madoc smiled a little. That would make the proud Roman even more anxious to catch up with the thieves. And it would give his runaway slave plenty of time in which to reach Gaza, trade the donkeys for food, and get aboard a ship for Italy. Once at Ancona, he could walk back to Cremona—and his mother! Somehow, then, the way would open to slip away with her into the forests that were home to them both!

"Perfect!" he shouted aloud. "I cannot fail!"

The dark-faced leader of the caravan came riding back along the line. He stared in amazement at the sight of the little yellow-haired stranger.

Madoc jumped to the ground. Still holding the ropes, he bowed.

"I have tried to make you hear, my lord," he explained, "but the sound of the bells was louder than my voice. Is it permitted that your servant ride with you to Gaza? I must go at once, and I—my master feared to have me ride alone through the desert."

It came so easily, sounded so smooth in his own ears, that Madoc was not surprised when the trader smiled.

"It is permitted, my son. Though I wonder why one so young should be traveling alone."

Madoc drew his lips closer. "I may not speak of my master's business that takes me to Gaza. I am his trusted servant."

The trader's sharp eyes studied him, much as Gratus had done at the slave market.

Madoc spoke quickly. "My master is Cornelius, the Roman centurion."

The caravan leader's face changed. "Ah, yes, I have heard of the brave centurion! When you return to him, tell him that Nabal the trader has befriended his servant."

Madoc mounted again. He would, he decided, work out every detail as he rode. There was plenty of time in which to plan.

They passed a village of dusty black tents, set up beside a water hole. No men were about, but the women and children came to watch the caravan. At sight of the white-skinned lad, they stared in wonder.

Madoc sighed. How alone he was, in this strange land, now that he had decided to leave his master and Hannibal! He thought of Orestes, waiting for him to come back, and his high spirits sank a little.

He reviewed in his mind his reasons for going. There was his vow. He must find and free his mother. Then his hatred for the Romans. He remembered the Roman soldiers in Gaul, and the guards who had driven him to the slave market. He thought of Gratus, shaking him like a rabbit. And the guard on shipboard, who had beaten his fellow countryman. And Cornelius! How many reasons he had for hating his master! Then somehow the words turned themselves about in his mind to make a question. How many reasons had he for hating his master?

He recalled every instance in which Cornelius had treated him harshly. He tried to remember every day of his slavery.

Picking them off one by one like grapes from the bunch, he came to the day at Joppa and the visit to the shop of Simon the tanner. That reminded him of the cake of pressed dates Cornelius had tossed to him and the stabbing pain that came again to his back.

The caravan was making its way across a dry river bed. Stiff-legged, the donkeys let themselves down the bank.

All at once Madoc lifted his head with a jerk, as if he had wakened suddenly. He glanced ahead at the weaving line of camels, then up at the afternoon sun.

"My lord Nabal!" he shouted. "I must go back! I—there is something of the greatest importance I have just remembered!"

It made no difference that the trader could not possibly hear. Madoc jumped from his donkey and snubbed both ropes about the stump of a dead oleander tree. He waited, breathing impatiently. He dared not loosen the ropes until the slow-moving camels had passed from sight above the opposite rim of the river bed.

He had come in his remembering to the night after leaving Joppa when he lay awake, sighing with pain. He was feeling again the touch of his master's fingers, cleansing and healing his wounded back.

He would send the letter, as he had planned. But he could not leave now—just when his master needed him most! There would be another, a better time for escape. He would wait for that.

CHAPTER 11: HYENAS!

When he could no longer hear the camel bells, Madoc
loosened the ropes. He turned the donkeys about, and they
followed willingly along the way they had come. He looked
at the sun. He was about three camel hours from the camp at
Hebron. But camels walked very slowly. If he hurried, he might
yet get back before his master. He strained at the ropes. After a
time, he found another guiding stick beside the highway and he
mounted.

It seemed much later when Madoc sighted the water
hole with the tent village beside it. As he came near, he saw
that women were coming from the tents to stand beside the
highway. They seemed to be waiting for him.

"I must not stop," he muttered, "Better to pass them as fast as
possible."

By the time he reached the group, he had urged and beaten
his donkeys into a steady little trot. But the women blocked
his way. Half a dozen hands reached out to catch the donkey's
ropes. Without speaking to him, they gathered about, laughing
and chattering.

"I must go at once," Madoc shouted. "My master is expecting
me at Hebron!"

For answer, the women looked at one another, still laughing. They ran their fingers through his hair, touched his bare arms, even pinched his cheek.

Madoc's face grew very red. "I pray you, let me pass," he cried. "My master, who is Cornelius the centurion, will not be pleased if you keep me here."

They had been treating him like an amusing child, but once again the name of his master did for him what he could not do for himself.

"Stay with us for the night," urged a smiling young woman who had a baby strapped in a little hammock across her back. "It is not safe for one so young to travel alone in the dark."

Madoc shook his head and tried to push on. Precious minutes were passing. The young woman spoke to a little boy who was standing nearby, peeping at Madoc through dirty brown fingers. The child ran to a tent and returned with an uncured sheepskin.

"Take this," said the girl with the baby. "If you must go, it will keep you warm when the heat of the sun has left the earth."

"I give you thanks," Madoc replied.

He had shaken the rope free of her hands when he noticed an old woman coming from one of the tents. She was leaning on a heavy stick. At sight of him she blinked and rubbed her eyes. Then she screamed, "Leper! Leper!" She hobbled forward, shaking her stick. "See, his skin is white! He is unclean!" she screeched. "Take your hands from him!"

Then to Madoc she shouted, "Away with you! Take with you
the curse that would kill us all!"

Now she was close beside him, her dim eyes wild with fear.
She lifted her stick and, with a scream of rage, brought it down
on first one donkey and then the other.

Away they went! Madoc clung with both hands and legs as
his donkey kicked and lunged. Each time the beast lifted his
heels, Madoc slipped forward a little farther until he was astride
the slender neck. For a moment he clung, weaving from side
to side. Then with a final kick, the donkey lowered his head.
Madoc slid off over his ears and rolled in the sand. The little
beast leaped over him and was gone.

Madoc got up. He looked after the racing animals, then
back at the village. The women and children were watching.
They shouted at one another, but they made no move to follow.
Gritting his teeth with anger, Madoc picked up the sheepskin
and started after the donkeys.

They were trotting now, southward across the desert. Madoc
ran. His breath came sharp as he tried to keep them in view.
Thorns swept against his ankles, but he did not bother to look
down. Now and again he glanced anxiously toward the sun.
When the donkeys stopped to nibble at the twigs of a gnarled
desert shrub, he took fresh courage. He crept forward.

The animals lifted their heads, long ears pricked toward him.
They waited and watched until a hand reached out to catch
at a dangling rope. Then, with a carefree flip of the tail, they

were off again across a deep gully and up to the top of a low, rock-strewn hill.

And so it went, until the hot, red sun dipped out of sight. Perhaps now they were tired, Madoc thought. With a last flicker of hope, he slipped behind a thornbush. He reached out for a rope that trailed through the sand, like a lazy brown serpent. The brush crackled under his knee. The rope slipped away, and the donkeys trotted up the slope of a flat-topped mound in the center of which was a huge pile of rocks.

Madoc stood perfectly still and shouted in a hoarse voice with rage. He watched until they disappeared behind the pile of rocks. Then he looked about. He could not see the tent village or any living thing. He was alone, and the night was upon him. Suddenly his mouth went dry. His knees bent under him. "It is because I have eaten nothing since morning," he muttered.

He broke off a twig and chewed the wood for its juice. He thought of the many nights he had spent alone in the forests of his homeland. But there had always been a tree to climb if wild boars threatened, or a cave in which one could be safe.

Madoc looked up at the strange jumble of stones behind which the donkeys had disappeared. Some were still piled one upon another, like the walls of a tower that long ago had fallen into ruin. Perhaps from the top of the heap he could see farther into the deepening gloom.

He hurried up the slope to the base of the pile. He fastened his sheepskin to his belt, then took off his sandals and hung them about his neck. His bare toes caught and clung to the crevices as he climbed up the steep side of the rock pile. On the topmost block he found a flattened surface on which he could stand.

Turning in every direction, Madoc strained his eyes to see. Then he closed them, the better to listen. Nothing! Not even the click of a locust or the chirp of a sleepy sparrow. The world was far away. He swayed with sudden dizziness, then sat to keep from crashing down the steep wall of rocks.

A chilling wind began to blow. Madoc shivered. Perhaps at the base of the pile he could find a cave or sheltered nook.

He let himself down again to the ground. He would look about while there was still a little light. A tiny black serpent crawled slowly into a crack between two rocks. With a small stick, Madoc clawed through the rubble that had blown against the base of a ruined wall. There he found bits of pottery, their broken edges worn smooth by the rubbing of sand and wind.

"People have lived here," he said aloud. The sound of his own voice was startling. He stood up and drew the sheepskin about his shoulders. There was still a faint glow in the western sky. He looked once more into the gathering shadows for a light that might point the way to an Arab tent. The wind grew stronger. It carried away all the warmth of the sun as it whistled through the crevices of the rocks.

Madoc huddled into the corner from which he had cleared the rubble. Now he was better able to cover himself with the sheepskin. He tucked it about his shoulder, the wool next to his body. He drew his feet up under his tunic and closed his eyes.

Perhaps if he could sleep he would forget the hunger that ached in his stomach and the fear that kept him shivering.

He was dreaming restlessly in the chill of midnight when suddenly he started up with a stab of terror. What was it? Something from his dream?

He listened, holding his breath. Out of the darkness it came again—a wild, echoing scream, and then another!

Madoc's body collapsed. Then he jerked himself up, his back pressed hard against the rocks. "Hyenas!" he gasped.

Again and again that blood-chilling sound! His ears found the direction from which it came—the dry river bed through which he had walked only a few hours before!

Once more the scream, now louder and nearer! Madoc's eyes opened wide, straining to see. He could hear his own breathing, shallow and quick. He got to his feet. Particles of sand, blowing against the rocks, sounded like the scratching of tiny claws.

Suddenly out of the darkness something took shape! In its midst was a pair of gleaming green eyes. Then another pair, and another!

They moved from side to side as the hideous brutes seemed to be swinging their heads back and forth, close to the ground. Madoc could hear a steady, rasping growl deep in their throats and the vicious chop of jaws as they lunged uneasily at one another. Now he could make out the dark outline of three slinking bodies. His eyes followed theirs as if under a spell.

The wind shifted, and a sickening musky odor reached his nose. The growling grew louder, but the beasts were moving more slowly. All at once Madoc realized it was because they were uncertain. There was the scent of the sheepskin tempting them forward, but the man smell made them hesitate. He remembered that Cornelius had said they were cowards! The thought gave him a flicker of hope.

Madoc tried to shout. His mouth opened, but no sound came. "The Lord is my shepherd!" he cried out in his heart, and it was a prayer.

The brutes had stopped. One pair of gleaming eyes was lowered, close to the ground. For a moment they were fixed, then the shadowy body edged forward, easing itself from side to side. He was settling for the spring!

Instantly something snapped inside Madoc's numbed brain. With a hoarse yell, he snatched the sheepskin from his shoulders and hurled it directly into the face of the crouching brute. Then he turned. Up, up the face of the rocks he went, almost as if he were flying! Below, he could hear the snarling and screaming of the hyenas. It churned into a hideous roar.

The sound drove Madoc upward with no feeling for bruised toes and skinned knees. His fingers caught the projecting rock edges; his toes found the niches as if guided by magic. And he landed safely, face downward on the top-most block.

There he lay, panting, his eyes closed. He listened to the snap of teeth and that rumbling, spitting roar. It turned his blood cold, and he drew his feet up sidewise over the rim of the rock.

All at once he noticed that the noise was growing less. It had settled down to an occasional growl, an ill-natured snap of powerful jaws. Then silence.

Madoc peered over the edge of the rock. His heart leaped again in panic. Were they coming? Climbing up as he had done?

He could see nothing. After a time he heard again that wild scream. It was not so loud, and it came from the direction of the river bed. Madoc's body grew suddenly limp. He shivered violently.

When he was able to think clearly again, he discovered that by lying flat the wind did not reach him as it did when he sat up. He settled himself into a more comfortable position and turned his face toward the east. Would the night ever end?

Sure that he could not sleep, he closed his eyes to wait. When he opened them again, the desert had begun to emerge from the darkness, and the hyenas were still.

For a time he lay quiet. His face and hair were wet with dew, and his tunic clung close to his shivering legs. Then the blinding red sun peered over the eastern hills and the dew arose like steam from a boiling kettle.

With stiffened legs and aching head, Madoc lowered himself to the ground. He looked back at the rock wall up which he had climbed in the dark. How had he ever done it without falling?

He blinked in the sunlight. "Is it possible that the God of Orestes is my shepherd?" he asked aloud.

Except for a few scattered shreds of wool, the sheepskin had entirely disappeared. He found a sheltered nook on the sunny side of the rocks and in a minute was sound asleep.

CHAPTER 12: STRANGE PUNISHMENT

Madoc wakened with a cry of terror. He leaped to his feet. Hyenas again? He blinked, confused at a sudden uproar close to his rocky shelter. Then he gasped with relief. It was the cheerful racket of barking dogs!

A shepherd, leading his flock, had passed close by without seeing him. But the dogs, coming along behind the sheep, had scented his hiding place.

The shepherd turned. Madoc fumbled down the slope. "Wait, sir," he shouted. "Wait, I pray you."

"Peace be with you," said the stranger, and Madoc knew such peace as had never filled his soul before. His voice was weak with relief as he came nearer.

"Oh, sir," he went on, "tell me the way to Hebron that I may return to my master, who is Cornelius the centurion."

The shepherd stared at Madoc's blood-stained legs and matted hair. "You have been all night in the desert?"

"Since yesterday at the noon hour, when my donkeys ran away to follow a caravan."

The dogs, still suspicious, sniffed at Madoc's bare legs. He drew closer to the shepherd, who spoke sharply to them.

"Come with me," said the man after thinking for a moment. "I cannot leave my flock to show you the way to Hebron. But in the evening you may go with me to the sheepfold. The way from there is plain."

Madoc was content not even to think as he trudged on beside the shepherd. Suddenly he realized that he was tired and thirsty and very, very hungry. The man gave him a drink from his leather water bottle, then reached into his knapsack.

"Here is bread," he said. "Take and eat as we walk together."

The flat unleavened loaf was hard and dry, but Madoc swallowed it quickly. As he plodded on, the shepherd called to the sheep in a slow monotonous singsong. Madoc, too weary to do more than drag his feet along, had nothing to say.

They reached the river bed from which the hyenas had come the night before. The path dropped down abruptly, then made its way northward with many a turn. Finally it brought them to a wide, level meadow. In it, grass and shrubs and oleander trees were still green.

The shepherd turned and spoke to the sheep. They stopped at once, every head turned toward him.

To Madoc he said, "Wait here with the flock."

He strode forward into the meadow. Madoc sat down to rest. After a time the shepherd called, and the sheep poured into their grazing ground.

"Sir," Madoc said uneasily, "It was from this direction that the hyenas came last night."

"I know that they are near," the shepherd answered, "But I have closed the mouths of their holes with rock. Now the sheep may graze in safety."

Limp with relief, Madoc lay down to rest in the shade of an oleander tree.

"In the presence of their enemies," he yawned. "The good shepherd has prepared a feast for his flock, even as in the song that Orestes taught me."

In the afternoon the shepherd roused Madoc, and they started back toward the east. They passed again the ruined tower where Madoc had spent the night. After a time they came to a low ridge of mountains which stretched from north to south across the desert. The shepherd followed a well-worn path. It led through a deep ravine and out again to the more level desert floor.

The sun was going down when Madoc saw before them the high stone wall of a sheepfold and the curb of a desert well. The shepherd pointed northward. "The road to Hebron," he said.

Madoc helped to draw water for the sheep as the shepherd called them, a few at a time, to drink from the stone trough. When the earthen jar had been raised for the last time, Madoc and the shepherd drank deeply.

"Sir," Madoc said as he wiped the water from nose and chin, "in my country the water is found in rivers and lakes. Is this the still water that is spoken of in the song to your God?"

The shepherd nodded and smiled warmly. "How is it that you, a stranger from a far land, have learned of my God?"

"I know little more than the song," Madoc admitted. "The song that tells how he cares for his people, as you have watched over your sheep today."

A small, faded black tent was stretched close by. A clay oven stood beside its entrance. When the sheep had been safely folded, the shepherd kneaded salt and water into meal to make thin flat loaves. Madoc gathered fuel to heat the oven. While the bread was baking, the man went into the sheepfold and returned with a jar full of milk. Madoc listened curiously as his new friend asked God's blessing upon the food. Then they sat down cross-legged to their meal of bread and cheese and milk.

All was quiet as the glow of sunset faded and with it the heat of the day. From the barren mountains eastward came the wail of a jackal.

Madoc's whole body grew warm with contentment. On the morrow there would be problems to face. But for tonight he was safe, well fed, and he had found a friend!

Suddenly the stillness was broken by the sound of galloping horses, coming from the south. Madoc leaped to his feet. He ran to the highway. Out of the shadows came a dozen horsemen. At their head rode Cornelius the centurion.

"Master!" screamed Madoc. Then he stopped. He stepped back. With bowed head and hands folded across his chest, he waited.

There was a moment of silence, tense and grim. Madoc's heart turned cold. The shepherd came to stand beside him in the gloom.

"Peace be with you," said his new friend to Cornelius. "This lad came to me in the desert, where he had become lost. I have cared for him. Now I entreat you, come also and sup in the tent of your servant, Ezra."

Madoc cast a quick glance at his master's face. It was lined and gray with dust. His eyes were red, his mouth drawn into a tight, thin line.

All at once Madoc's spirits lifted. Cornelius had not sent his men into the desert to find a lost slave. He had gone himself to lead them in the search!

As Madoc watched, the centurion's frown faded a little. He drew a deep, tired breath, as if he would gladly get down and rest. Then he asked, "How is it that you, a Jew, would break bread with a Gentile? Is that not contrary to your law?"

The shepherd answered, "I am indeed a Jew, a Bethlehemite. But have you not heard of the new law that has come to us from the Master?"

Before the Roman could answer, he added proudly, "I am a follower of the new Way."

Madoc saw the centurion's tight lips relax. "Go on to Hebron," he called to the men who waited behind him. "Our search is ended. I shall return to camp on the morrow."

The soldiers urged their horses forward as Cornelius followed the shepherd into the tent.

Although his master had not spoken to him, Madoc was content to sit in the shadows and watch and listen.

"Good shepherd," said Cornelius when he had eaten, "will you tell me something of your God and of this new way of living? I have heard a little, and it interests me strangely."

A fire had been built in the middle of the tent. Cornelius gazed for a moment at the crackling thorns. Then he confessed, "I have tried to put the matter out of my mind, but I can think of little else."

The shepherd's eyes grew thoughtful, as if he were remembering the face of one deeply loved. "You say you have heard?"

Cornelius replied, "In Caesarea word came to me from a learned Greek. In Joppa I learned from Simon the tanner something of this strange new Way."

The shepherd thought for a moment, then he said, "There would not be time, though I talked all through the night, to tell you of the Savior, of his healings and teachings that would make all men happy if they would but listen and obey."

It was not the way of the proud Roman to obey anyone, and Madoc saw his master frown. Then he said, "But this question puzzles me, good shepherd. There are so many gods! We Romans worship our emperor in addition to all the rest. How is it that you have only one God and find him able to satisfy all your needs?"

The shepherd looked grave. "My lord," he answered, "living in the wilderness one has much time to think. And I have come to believe that when the unbelievers call upon the gods of Greece and Rome, they are searching for the living God, whose name they know not."

Madoc could see that Cornelius was startled, but the shepherd went on. "I was a lad," he said, "living in Bethlehem on the night that our Savior was born."

He got up and threw more brush into the fire. Then he sat down and stared into the heart of the flames. "Those of us who were there will never forget. Think you that we who have seen and known a living Savior could ever look upon an image, or into the face of a sinful man, and call him God?"

Madoc looked at his master through the smoke that clouded the tent. Cornelius' face was confused and doubtful.

Madoc went outside, for the smoke hurt his eyes. He sat down to watch a cold half-moon ride slowly across the sky. He shivered as he listened to the talk that went on and on in question and answer. Finally he went to sleep.

Sometime later he realized that he was being lifted and that his head rested on a broad chest. But it was not the worn sheepskin of the shepherd's mantle against which his cheek rubbed. Rather, there was a familiar odor of horses and new leather. Then he was laid on a bed of sheepskins and covered warmly. Once again he was strangely happy.

At break of day Madoc was roused by the bleating of sheep.

The shepherd had left the tent, but in the faint light Madoc could see the huddled form of his master under a mound of sheepskins beside him.

There was a hurried breakfast, then Cornelius mounted his horse. Madoc waited, both fearful and eager.

"Take your place behind me," snapped the centurion. It was the first time he had spoken to his slave. Madoc lost no time in clambering up behind the saddle.

Cornelius turned to the shepherd. "I thank you for the care you have given my servant. And to me also you have given much."

"In the town of Lydda," said Ezra, "there lives a man named Eneas. He is learned in the teachings of Jesus. He could help you to understand better than I. Go, in the peace of God."

It was a long, silent ride back to camp. As they rode up the slope of the tents, Hannibal came running to catch the reins of the sweating horse. His white teeth flashed as he caught sight of Madoc's humped figure, nearly hidden behind the broad back of the centurion.

As they walked behind their master, the African looked down at Madoc and scowled fiercely. "Now we shall see what comes of your running away!"

Madoc gave no sign that he had heard.

"Come into the tent," Cornelius called over his shoulder.

Madoc obeyed. He was feeling a little sick inside.

The centurion was walking back and forth. He did not look up as he said, "Now from the beginning I want the story of your disobedience and what befell you in the desert."

Madoc stood just inside the curtained doorway. He would not hang his head. Instead, he fixed his eyes on a plump new bulge in the wall of the tent. He was sure it was Hannibal, listening outside. As his master ordered, he told everything that befell. His thoughts, that had tempted him to go on with the caravan, were his own. They belonged to the part of him that could never be enslaved.

When his story was finished Cornelius said, "Call Hannibal."

The bulge in the tent disappeared, and the African came before Madoc had time to call.

"In the camp of a soldier," said Cornelius, "disobedience must be punished." He turned to Hannibal. His voice was cold and stern. "Take this disobedient servant and give him ten lashes with the bull whip."

Madoc glanced up. The dark face beside him twisted as if with pain. Hannibal seemed unable to move.

"At once!" snapped the centurion.

The two backed through the tent doorway. Madoc could hear a low moaning growl in the throat of his fellow slave.

"Hannibal!"

That unhappy servant jumped, then turned to attention. Madoc too looked back into their master's stern face.

"Bear in mind that the lad's back has recently been wounded. I will have you beaten if his hurt is broken open anew."

Hannibal bowed and backed completely out of the tent. He was grinning broadly now. And the growl that came from his throat was more like the purr of a contented cat.

CHAPTER 13: A MAD DOG

In the days that followed, Madoc made good use of his time. He smiled with secret contentment as he looked over the growing pile of pottery pieces on which he had copied the words he would need for his letter.

"Almost enough," he whispered, "to make her know that I live and that I have not forgotten my vow."

Sometime in the night he was roused as Cornelius came into the tent.

"Help me remove my helmet and breastplate," said his master.

Madoc forced his eyes to stay open as he stumbled to his feet. "Yes, my lord."

"Bring me bread and meat and cool water."

"The bread and meat are here, my lord, in a covered dish. I will bring the water from the jar outside."

He held the bowl while Cornelius washed his face and hands. Then, almost too tired to eat, the centurion held out his hand for the bread.

"We leave on the morrow," he said. "Tell Faduel to buy two more donkeys in the town. Do not disturb me until I waken."

He yawned as his head dropped back on the pillow. "The
Arabs have gone. And I am weary enough to sleep the night and
day through."

Madoc got up early next morning. He took his stand in front
of his master's tent. He allowed no one to come near, lest the
centurion be disturbed. The other tents were all down, the camp
equipment packed before Cornelius called for his breakfast.

Madoc learned that they were going directly to Lydda. Could
it be that his master was impatient to see the learned teacher,
Eneas, of whom the shepherd had spoken?

It was pleasant, after the heat of the desert, to ride through
orchards of olive and fig and pomegranate, to rest in the shade
of mulberry and sycamore. The wheat harvest in the hill country
was a few weeks later than it had been on the southern plains.

"These are more like the harvest fields of my homeland,"
Madoc said to Hannibal. His voice shook a little. "Only a year
ago I watched as the servants of my father cut the yellow stalks
and bound them into sheaves."

Hannibal, from the back of his jogging donkey, glanced
across at Madoc's downcast face. "Eh, lad, you have small cause
to look down at your nose. You have been many months in the
house of our master and only once have you been flogged." He
grinned. "And don't say that Hannibal hurt you! Not even with
the bruise on your back!"

Madoc laughed a little, then his face grew sad again. "'Tis not
that the master has been unkind, Hannibal. It is a feeling here."
He laid a hand across his chest. "It is the pain of remembering."

Hannibal rubbed the back of his neck as he hunted for the words he wanted to say. "Slaves have nothing to remember."

Madoc answered sharply, "I shall never forget my mother! And some day I shall go to free her from the chains that hold her to the loom!"

Hannibal's dark eyes rolled in fear. "Don't run away, lad! Hannibal be obliged to flog you if you do! Don't run away from the master who loves you!"

"Loves me?" Madoc laughed at the worried look on the face of the big man beside him. "Today I shall not run away. Have no fear. But some day I shall go free! It is a promise that I have made, and I have prayed to God—"

"To the god that most burned the skin off your face in the desert?"

"No, Hannibal. It has come to my ears that there is another God—a God who wants his followers to do good to their enemies."

Hannibal was interested at once. "Something hard to understand about that," he mused, "how are people ever going to have any wars if all of them do good to their enemies?"

Hannibal rubbed the back of his neck as he thought.

"How are people going to have any enemies to be good to?" he asked.

"Hannibal," Madoc exclaimed, "it may be that is just what this good God hopes will come to pass!"

For a time they rode on without speaking. Then Madoc
asked, "But why do you say that our master loves me, Hannibal?
Why would he love a slave that he has bought with money?"

The African grinned. "He was most ready to flog Hannibal
when he came back to camp and found you were gone. And
did he not tell me to lay the whip on lightly—not to break
your skin?"

Madoc was set to thinking. He remembered the strange, glad
feeling that had come to him when his master appeared at the
sheepfold. He recalled the thrill of relief that he felt every night
when the centurion came back to camp unhurt.

Hannibal broke into his thoughts. "Nearly to the town, lad,
where we camped before. See, yonder are the trees."

Madoc jumped from his donkey and raced ahead on foot,
in order to be there first. He darted among the trees, looking to
the right and left. Between two giant sycamores he found the
coolest, shadiest spot in the whole grove.

He ran to meet the oncoming caravan. "Hannibal!" he
shouted, "I have found the place for our master's tent. Come
and help me mark off the ground!"

There was much to do in the sycamore grove as tents were
raised and their stakes pounded down with Hannibal's huge
wooden mallet. Madoc was starting to the brook for water
when Cornelius arrived.

"Leave the water carrying to others," he called to Madoc.
"Come with me into the town."

Very cheerfully the water jar was returned to the cook tent. Madoc walked behind his master along the highway. It led them past the homes of the poor—miserable little hovels made of loose stones, piled one upon another. They had been gathered, Madoc decided, from the ruins of other houses that stood all about, roofless and broken.

A part of the city's wall was still standing, but as they came near, Madoc could see that the gates were broken down. Great heaps of stones lay tumbled about.

A group of lepers sat among the broken rocks, well back from the roadside. "Unclean, unclean," they wailed.

Madoc looked into their white, sick faces and turned away.

Beside the ruined gate a crippled beggar crouched in the midst of the rubble. "My lord the centurion," he whined. "A penny, I pray you, in the name of Jesus!"

Cornelius stopped abruptly. "What do you, a beggar, know of him?"

"Very little, my lord," the crippled man hastened to say. "In truth, nothing at all, except what has been told to me by others who know him."

"And what was told to you?"

The beggar's voice lost its whine. "That when he was here among men, Jesus said to his followers, 'Blessed are the merciful.'"

Cornelius tossed a coin and the beggar caught it expertly. Then he called down a blessing upon the giver, who walked on, frowning.

Inside the gate the litter of ruined houses nearly choked the narrow way. A wild dog, lying in the sun, got up with a snarl as they came near, and disappeared among the ruins.

Madoc saw two old men walking toward them. He took them to be Jews, for they were dressed in long, loose robes, fringed at the edges. Their heads were covered with squares of red and blue cloth, held in place by scarves wound about them.

The men stepped aside as the Roman came near. In their downcast eyes Madoc saw a look of hatred.

Cornelius, however, stopped them. "Tell me, good sirs, where I may find the house of Eneas, the scholar."

The two men looked not at all at the Roman, but into each other's bearded faces. Finally one of them said, "We know him not." Then they walked past, their eyes still turned away.

Madoc looked up. His master's hand was on his sword, his face flushed with anger. Then suddenly he muttered, "With their homes laid in ruins, they have reason enough to hate."

Madoc understood. It was the Romans who had laid waste to the city!

A boy, chasing sparrows from the uncovered baskets of a fruit merchant, was more friendly. Or perhaps, Madoc thought, more in awe of the long sword that swung from the leather belt

of the centurion. As the boy led the way, Madoc noticed that his
dangling hands were like the claws of a bird, and his head much
too large for his body. They had come to the foot of a hill, and
the boy lifted a skinny arm to point the way. Before he hurried
back to the market place, he stared directly at Madoc. His
face was like a mask, but it was easy for Madoc to see that the
thoughts it hid were ugly.

Startled, Madoc looked after him. He heard the boy call
shrilly as he reached the fruit stall. Was his shout intended to
chase the sparrows away, or had it another purpose?

Cornelius had started up the hill. Madoc ran to overtake
him, forgetting the boy in the market place. The centurion
stopped in front of a white stone house that stood on the hill
slope, in the midst of a garden.

"Wait here." Cornelius said to Madoc, and he walked up the
shell-paved path.

In answer to his knock, a window in the second story was
opened. Then, at sight of the Roman, it was closed again.

Cornelius waited. Suddenly the door swung wide. A Jew, in
the long mantle of his people, stood before the centurion. Even
at a distance, his face was somehow familiar to Madoc.

Cornelius asked, "Are you Eneas, the scholar?"

"I am he."

Madoc heard his master suggest that they talk in the
garden, since he knew the Jewish custom that forbade the

presence of unbelievers in their homes. But the Jew stepped inside and invited Cornelius inside. He was welcoming the Roman to his home!

Out in the desert it had seemed the natural thing for a shepherd to invite a tired traveler into his tent. But now the Jewish scholar had done the same. It was indeed a strange new way!

Madoc leaned against the trunk of an oak tree. He was thinking. Suddenly he said aloud, "I will do it! I will give it a trial!"

"Ho!" shouted a jeering voice close behind the tree. "No one will speak to the slave of a Roman, and so he talks to himself!"

Madoc turned sharply. His face was very red. He was about to shout an angry threat. Then he stopped. Here at once was a chance to make trial of the new Way.

Led by the lad from the market place, a group of boys had come up quietly. Madoc counted five of them. Their looks were far from friendly as they came around the tree to face him.

"Peace be with you," Madoc said.

The boy from the market place grinned unpleasantly. He mimicked Madoc's friendly tone. "And peace be with you, white face!"

He turned to the others who stood beside him. "See, did I not tell you that his face is like a leper's? And look at his nose, speckled like a bird's egg!"

"I have come from a far land," Madoc explained. "There the light of the sun is gentler. It does not brown the skin as it does here."

"White skin! Spotty face!" shouted another. "Slave of a Roman! Go back to the place where the sun is cold!"

Madoc's good humor served only to anger them. Suddenly a stone thrown with accurate aim struck his shoulder. Again it was the boy from the market place! The others, frightened by their leader's daring, ran away down the hill.

Madoc leaped forward, an angry flush blazing into his face. The leader faced him defiantly. Then his courage broke and he turned to follow the others.

As he raced away, he stumbled and fell flat in the dust of the road. Instantly came a snarl as a wild dog leaped from the wayside hedge.

Madoc screamed. He kicked at the beast, just as he sank his teeth into the shoulder of the fallen boy. The boy gave a shriek of pain and terror. Then Madoc's fingers closed about the dog's throat.

The body writhed under his hands, then slowly the slavering jaws relaxed. Madoc flung the beast, kicking and slashing, away to the roadside. But the dog seemed to recover, almost in mid-air. He turned upon Madoc, snarling in fury.

"Get up!" Madoc snapped to the boy at his feet. But the boy did not move, except to press his arms closely about his head. With every breath came a moan of panic.

Now the dog circled the two, lips drawn back from gleaming white teeth. Madoc turned to face him. "Begone!" he shouted.

The dog crouched. He eyed the boy on the ground. Madoc could see that the taste of blood had maddened the beast. The dog's body grew tense. His tongue curled, jaws dripping.

"Master!" Madoc screamed with all the power of his lungs. "Master, come! Help! Help!"

The dog quivered, ready to spring. Then Madoc heard a door open suddenly, a shout behind him, and racing along the path. He dared not turn, but in a sidelong glance he saw Cornelius.

A drawn sword flashed. The dog leaped aside, then slunk away, still snarling.

Madoc's legs turned suddenly weak. He swayed as Cornelius placed a firm hand on his shoulder.

Eneas, the Jew, followed close behind. He helped the wounded boy to his feet. And now Madoc knew him. Eneas was the man who had stood between himself and Aaron, the goatherd, at the brookside!

"They are like jackals, these dogs," said Eneas. "They have nothing to eat, save the refuse of the town. The beast must have been mad with hunger, for they are cowardly and seldom attack."

He clapped his hands, and a servant came to care for the wounded boy.

"There is much more that I would ask," said Cornelius as they stood beside the door. "I will come again. I am moved to

renounce the gods of my people. I shall try, through prayer and
the giving of alms, to find favor with your God."

As they stood and talked, the servant returned with the
injured boy. Madoc saw that the blood had been washed from
his shoulder and that a clean white cloth covered the wound.

Side by side he and Madoc walked down the path behind the
centurion. When they reached the roadside, the boy stooped
and picked up a small stone. Then he straightened himself and
turned to look at Madoc. His brows drew together in a fierce
scowl. "When I throw a stone," he boasted, "it lands on its mark."

Madoc rubbed his bruised shoulder. "That I know to be
true."

They walked on. A goat, feeding in a nearby yard, lifted its
head as they came near.

The boy looked up again with his threatening frown. "Look
here!" He lifted his arm. "If anyone ever dares to say that your
skin is like a leper's, or that your nose is spotted, I shall treat
him to this!"

The stone flashed through the air. It landed directly between
the eyes of the astonished goat!

They were nearing the market place. The boy turned for a
last meaningful frown at Madoc. "Remember!" Then he darted
away.

All at once Madoc's whole body grew warm with happiness.
The flush mounted even into his face. His plan had worked!
And his enemy, whose life he had saved, no longer hated him!

He stared for a moment at the marching feet and swinging sword before him. "I," he announced to nobody but himself, "am a follower of the Way!"

At the market place, the centurion stopped before a booth where a man was sitting on the ground under a shelter of palm branches. In the merchant's lap was a woven tray of round, flat loaves. Madoc watched with astonishment as Cornelius reached into his moneybag. He drew out a handful of coins.

"Give me bread of the worth of these denarii."

The merchant stared, loose-jawed. Suddenly he pushed the tray toward Cornelius. "You may have it all—all!"

Then a look of shrewdness passed over his face. "Except for a few loaves that I must take home to my children."

The centurion made no attempt to bargain, and the bread was piled into Madoc's arms. Two dogs, sniffing hungrily, crept closer to lick up any crumbs that might fall. The merchant shouted, and they backed away. Madoc looked at their hollow flanks, loosely covered with coarse-haired skin. His heart stirred in pity.

"You are sorry for these vicious beasts?" Cornelius asked.

Madoc started, embarrassed that his master had been watching him.

"I was thinking," he confessed, "that perhaps they would not be vicious if they were not crazed with hunger."

They went next to the fish market. Again the centurion

reached into his purse. He bought fish—much, much fish—and had it placed in a basket of woven reeds.

To Madoc he said, "We will take the fish away from the market before we give it to the dogs."

They had no difficulty persuading the dogs to follow. Indeed, their number grew rapidly. Madoc's bare legs kept him close to his master as he heard the snarling and sniffing behind.

They walked to the place of ruined houses just inside the city gate. There Madoc stopped beside the tumbled walls of what had once been a modest home.

"Now," said Cornelius, "let us give them such a meal as they have not known in all their lives before."

Madoc clambered onto the broken wall. Cornelius handed the heavy basket up to him and bade him toss the fish into the space beyond. Instantly the dogs were over the wall. Madoc laughed aloud as they fell upon the food with savage eagerness.

"Come," said the centurion, "let us hurry away, lest they follow again. The bread is not for them."

The cripple still lay in the shade outside the gate. Madoc handed him a generous portion of the hard wheat loaves. His cries of thanksgiving roused the lepers who lay sleeping in the sun, their tattered garments covering their pasty white faces.

"Leave the bread by the roadside," Cornelius told Madoc, "then come away quickly."

The Roman mused aloud as they hurried on, "Strange indeed it is to hear the voices of men raised in blessing instead of cursing." Then he muttered, "Strange, and pleasant to the ears."

Madoc looked toward the creek. Aaron was there. He was just leaving, after having watered his goats.

"Good master," Madoc called softly, "see, there is the goatherd with whom I fought! May your servant be permitted to run to him for a moment? I would return the slingshot he gave to me."

"Go at once!" replied the centurion.

The sun was setting when Madoc returned to camp. To him, the sky was indeed rose-colored, though the slingshot no longer dangled from his belt. With a plea for pardon, he had offered it. Aaron, poking embarrassed toes deep into the sand, had refused to take it. But Madoc had thrust it into his girdle and run away.

When he reached the top of the hill, Madoc looked back. Aaron was watching. As if at a given signal, both boys had raised a hand in friendly farewell.

CHAPTER 14: A HARD BARGAIN

The next day the caravan started on the last lap of its homeward bound journey. Madoc was glad to leave his donkey at the barracks and to walk with Hannibal back to the pleasant villa.

The following morning Madoc was sent to announce their return to Orestes and to resume his lessons.

"You have done well," the Greek told him when he wrote on the wax tablet all the words he had learned. "It is not the method by which one ordinarily learns to write—the difficult words first and then the easier and less important."

He eyed Madoc thoughtfully. "It seems almost as if you planned to use these words for a certain purpose of your own. In any case, it is a way that goes well for you. I hope your master will not disapprove."

Madoc drew his breath sharply. Orestes was warning him! It would be foolhardy to rouse any unnecessary suspicion.

"If it please you, my lord, I shall not write the name of my mother on the copy that I prepare for my master. And perhaps it would be wise to leave out one or two other words, as well."

The white head close above his own nodded agreement.

"Remember, in the eyes of Orestes you are not a slave. Write what you wish."

When his teacher was about to leave, Madoc asked, "Sire, have you a bit of papyrus on which I can in time write all the words I have learned?"

"I have indeed," the Greek replied, and he smiled.

Madoc did not explain that the papyrus was needed to write a letter, but he suspected that Orestes guessed as much. Madoc did not expect the Syrian peddler to return for several weeks, but it was well to have everything ready.

As time went on, Madoc watched for signs of the changing season. The months of extreme heat passed, and one day he said to Anna, "The mornings are cool and cloudy. Is it not coming near to the time of rains?"

The new crop of olives had been harvested, and the serving woman was busy with the pickling. She looked up, her hands wet with brine.

"Why is it you ask so often about the rains? I would say they will come in one or two weeks. Now make haste to the market place. I need more salt for the olives."

Madoc placed the moneybag into his knapsack as he walked along. The peddler had said, "A penny here, a penny there." Now that he was trusted to go alone to market, it was surprising how many small coins slipped from his master's purse to hide in the corners of his knapsack. Yet Madoc was not happy about taking the money. It always left an empty feeling in the middle of his chest, as if he himself were losing more than his master. He ate but poorly, and Cornelius complained that he muttered in his sleep.

Madoc purchased the salt and was turning to go home. Then, coming along the highway from the north, he saw a dust-clouded caravan of donkeys. He stopped and watched until he caught the flash of gold earrings in the sun. The Syrian peddler had returned!

Madoc forgot about Anna and the salt as he ran to greet the man. "Sir," he shouted, "the letter! I am ready to write it now!"

The Syrian's greedy eyes studied Madoc's face. "And the money? You have saved enough to pay me?"

"Oh, yes, my lord!" Madoc dug into his knapsack for the loose coins. "See, here are two denarii!"

The peddler frowned darkly. "Two denarii for delivering a letter to a town across the sea?"

Madoc's face lost all its light. "But sir, my master pays only one, and he is considered most generous. I cannot give you more!"

The man's lips turned down in an ugly grin. "Are there not three denarii there in your master's purse?"

Madoc shrank back. "No, no, I must not! Already I have taken too much!"

The peddler shrugged and turned away. "If you care so little for your mother, I have not time—"

"Wait!" Madoc pleaded. He was thinking aloud. "There may be a way, but I know not if I could! On the morrow, my master will send me with alms for the poor."

"Excellent!" cried the Syrian, and again his voice was friendly. "No beggar would question the amount of a gift, or tell it to your master."

Madoc's whole body grew tight with struggle in his mind. His throat was dry as he muttered, "But I would see their faces, their hunger! Oh, I cannot steal from the poor!"

Now the peddler's tone was oily, smoothing the way for Madoc's decision. "But your mother, is she not also poor and unhappy? Living without hope?"

Madoc nodded slowly, his head downcast. His hands trembled, and he swallowed to ease the tightness in his throat. "I will see you on the morrow. And—I will bring the money with the letter."

He started away with sagging steps, then he remembered Anna and hurried. She would be angry at his delay. He burst through the garden gate and took the salt to the kitchen.

Anna boxed his ears smartly. "Now go to your lessons! Your teacher is waiting in the garden. Would you have the master punish us both for your wasted time?"

The lesson went badly. Madoc's hand shook when he tried to write and he forgot to answer when he was asked a question.

At last Orestes laid down the tablet and stylus. "Your mind is far away, my son. Tell me—what troubles you?"

Madoc's muddled thoughts took shape. "It is a thing of right and wrong, my lord. I must first do the wrong before the good can be done."

Orestes reached out to touch his knee. "No good ever grows out of wrong, my son. You have told me that you are a follower of the Way. Have you asked God to help you decide?"

Madoc shook his head. "It is of no use. Though it burns in my stomach like a fire of thorns, I yet must do the wrong."

"What is this sin that you would do?"

Madoc's body sagged. He whispered, "I have stolen from my master's purse two denarii, and now I must steal even more from the poor!"

"That you may not do, my son. Give back what you have taken from the purse of Cornelius, and steal no more. It is written in the law of God: 'Thou shalt not steal.'"

Madoc swayed on the stone bench. So the matter had been decided for him? He lifted dull eyes to meet the pitying gaze of his teacher. "If I do not, then all my planning must come to nothing, and my mother—" his body shook with helpless sobs.

Orestes reached out an arm to steady the heaving shoulders. "You have not told me, lad, how much it is that you planned to steal."

"I must have five denarii." Madoc's voice sank to a whisper. "But you are right, my lord, I cannot take it."

The old man's body seemed to swell with the long breath that he drew into his lungs. "Lad, lad, I have it!"

Bony fingers probed into his own flat purse. "Give back what you have already taken! Here, count it! Two, three, five denarii. The generous wage that your good master has paid me!"

Madoc looked down at the silver coins in his open palm. All at once his face grew red with delight. His fingers closed over the money. "You—you give it to me?"

Orestes patted his flat stomach. "See! Your teacher grows fat with much eating, my son! I need not eat so much. Take the money, with God's blessing."

Madoc mumbled. "I fear I should not—but I know that I must!" Suddenly he dropped to his knees and kissed the hands of his friend.

That night Madoc waiting in shivering excitement until he was sure that Cornelius was sleeping soundly. Then, cautiously, he pushed his cloak aside and crept out of bed. On tiptoe he slipped out of the room and to the library.

A night lamp was kept always burning on a high pedestal. Madoc lifted it from its place and set it on the table. He reached for his master's reed pen and jug of ink. His hand trembled as his lips moved. "Please, God, let not my master waken and find me gone from my bed."

From the front of his tunic, Madoc took the scrap of papyrus that Orestes had given him. It was discolored and paper-thin from having been used and sponged so many times.

The letter had been worked out in Madoc's mind to the last detail. He formed the words with his lips as he dipped pen into ink and wrote:

"Madoc, your son, a servant of Cornelius the centurion at Caesarea in the province of Judea, to Greta, a slave in the mill of Julius the weaver. Greetings!

How many times had he scratched those words on his wax tablet, only to rub them out quickly with his thumb! Now they flowed in trembling eagerness from the tip of his master's pen, not to be erased! He could see the light in his mother's face as she read, and chills of excitement chased up and down his back.

He wrote on: "Have courage! Some day I shall come to set you free. I wait and pray to the God—"

"Madoc!"

In the stillness of midnight the voice of his master was to Madoc like the crack of Gratus' bull whip. He jumped. The reed pen fell from his fingers. It made a crazy black line as it rolled across the face of his letter.

"Put the lamp back on its stand, the pen and ink on the shelf. I have commended you for earnest study, but this is not the time for it."

From his place in the doorway Cornelius held out his hand. "Give me the papyrus on which you were writing."

Madoc's stomach turned sick. His head swam until he could not see clearly. So, after all, it was not to be. In the deathlike

silence that followed, he recalled the hours of study, his plans
and hopes for the letter, and Orestes' glad sacrifice. Now, like
the plaid cloak, all had crumbled into ashes. He could feel
the stern eyes of his master as with stiff fingers he put away
ink and pen, then the lamp. Last of all, Madoc picked up the
ink-smeared papyrus and placed it in his master's outstretched
hand.

CHAPTER 15: DISAPPOINTMENT

Madoc spent the rest of the night in a fever of despair. For many months the letter had been hidden in his heart, a precious thing. Now his heart ached with its loss. He listened as his master turned restlessly and finally muttered, "I'll do it!"

Madoc wondered what it was that the Roman had decided to do. Could it mean the awl through his ear? Or the bull whip? Even that would be welcome, if it would give him a chance to beg the privilege of sending even a small part of the letter.

But the next morning the eyes of his master were turned from Madoc, and he dared not speak. He was sent as usual to the market place. One small hope was left. The peddler was waiting. Madoc greeted him with downcast eyes. "I have no letter. It—was taken from me. Only this I can do."

He drew from his knapsack a small piece of checkered woolen cloth. It was soiled and scorched around the edges.

"If you could drop this into my mother's lap as you pass her loom—"

The peddler sneered at the worthless scrap of cloth. Madoc went on less hopefully. "It is a part of the cloak she made for me, long ago. She would know it came from me."

The Syrian growled, "And you expect me to take this, without pay?"

Madoc reached again into the knapsack. "Here is the money—five denarii. Perhaps you could whisper into her ear that someday—someday I will come!"

Madoc turned blindly and ran away. He did his errands as quickly as possible, then turned homeward. At the fountain in the courtyard he held out his hands for the plump little cherub to fill with water. Then he pressed them against his reddened eyes. In the kitchen Anna looked at him sharply, but she said nothing.

Later she warned Madoc, "Mind that you do not disturb the master. He is writing letters to go by the boat today."

Ah, yes, the master's letters would go! The master was a centurion, not a slave!

Madoc ate his bread and cheese with a dry throat. The sweet cake Anna gave him was, he knew, intended to cheer him, but he pushed it away and ran from the kitchen.

Life settled back into its even pattern of work and study. Cornelius said no word more about the letter. The boat that sailed without it was the last to leave port before the winds of winter made travel dangerous. As the days grew shorter, heavy draperies were drawn across the doorways, and Reuben brought into the house big three-legged brass bowls in which he kindled glowing fires of charcoal.

The early rains were well along when Madoc noticed that

Orestes' thin shoulders were growing more stooped. His lips were gray and tight, as if with pain. One day he came leaning on a stick.

At Madoc's anxious question, he answered, "'Tis a stiffness of the joints that comes with the rains." Then he smiled a little. "One must expect the pains of age. It is nothing."

But on the following day he did not come at the usual hour. Cornelius bade Madoc go to the little mud house under the aqueduct where Orestes lived alone.

At the sound of his pupil's voice the Greek called out, "Enter! I was hoping you would come, lad. I did not want your lessons interrupted by the weakness of an old man."

From his low couch he raised himself on one elbow. "Have you brought stylus and tablet, that we may go on without delay?"

Madoc came closer. "My master said that first I should ask about your health and if you are able to have me stay."

"If I am able," the old man repeated smiling. "In very truth, I am not able to lie here all day with nothing for company but my own small troubles. Come, lad, I can see the outline of the wax tablet hidden under your tunic. Let us get on at once with the lesson."

At the end of the week Cornelius called upon Madoc to read. The centurion nodded with approval. "Some day," he said, "you will be a scholar like Orestes. Your learning would be wasted in the camp of a soldier."

Madoc's heart thumped. Why was it, he wondered, that
nothing more had been said about the letter? Cornelius knew
now that he had planned, all along, to escape. Had the Roman,
because of that, decided to sell him? Was he going on with the
education of a slave so that he could make a greater profit on
the sale?

Madoc waited uneasily. He listened to the steady patter
of the rain and the drip of the water that trickled down from
the roof to fall in the pool in the front room. He flushed as he
felt the gaze of the centurion upon him. Somehow he felt that
Cornelius was thinking about the letter. Perhaps he was also
wondering what should be done with a slave boy who dared not
only for his own freedom but for the escape of another, too.

Madoc looked up in a quick glance. A frown deepened
between his master's narrowed eyes.

"I wonder," Cornelius muttered, "what is best to be done!"
Then he jumped to his feet and walked away.

Madoc watched the swinging folds of his master's mantle
until it disappeared through the curtained doorway. So
Cornelius did intend to do something! Would his ear be pierced
with the awl to make it harder for him to escape? He cringed at
the thought. Then his chin went up. Nothing could make him
forget his vow to his mother.

During the winter Cornelius was often called out with his
soldiers to settle quarrels or put down small rebellions. Madoc
was very sure that the people no longer need fear injustice
from his master. And though he knew he had given his master

cause for anger, he soon ceased to worry about the awl, for now Cornelius was always kind. Madoc could see that he was really trying to follow the new Way.

Every morning Madoc and Hannibal took baskets of food to the poor. Their words of blessing and thanksgiving poured out as freely as the rain. All this change in his master was, he knew, a part of the new way of living. And, though his most precious possession had been taken from him, he could not hate the man who owned him.

In the afternoons Madoc went to Orestes' little house for his lessons. And so his days were filled as the long winter months dragged by.

It was on a morning in early spring that Madoc went as usual to the mud hut under the Roman aqueduct. As he came near, he heard the voice of Orestes raised in song. It was the song that Anna and Reuben sang on the Sabbath.

Madoc waited outside to listen. "'The Lord is my light,'" sang Orestes. "'Whom shall I fear?'"

It reminded Madoc of the shepherd's song he had learned many months ago. He had not thought of that song for a long time. It meant little to him now. He was convinced that the God to whom Orestes and his master prayed was not for him. All of his faith in the new Way he had poured out in his prayer that night in his master's library. It had not been answered.

The old man's voice went on: "'Teach me the way, O Lord, and lead me in a plain path!'"

Madoc stepped into the doorway. "My lord," he burst out, "why do you sing to God? He may listen to the prayers of important people, like Cornelius, but do you think he is mindful of such as you and me?"

Orestes looked up through eyes grown dim with pain. His thin face was a network of wrinkles as he smiled. "The way of the Lord is for all who will walk in it, my son."

Madoc frowned at him through narrowed eyes. "Has he given light to your eyes, or taken the pain from your bones?"

Orestes looked back into Madoc's frowning eyes. "I did not ask for that. He has given me peace and hope in the days of my weakness." He paused, but Madoc did not answer. Then he went on, "I have waited and prayed that you might speak, my son. Since the day I gave you the five denarii, I have noticed that something was troubling you. I have noticed, too, that certain words have been left out of your writing."

Still Madoc made no reply. He stood with the gifts from Cornelius still in his arms. His eyes were fixed on the bare mud wall of the hut.

"Long ago," said Orestes, "the words of Jesus were told to me by one who in his youth had walked with the Master. Now listen, for I hid the words in my heart and have never forgotten them. 'Come unto me,' said Jesus, 'all ye that labor and are heavy laden—'"

Without a word, Madoc put down at Orestes' feet the food he had brought and ran from the house.

"I know not what to think of this new God," he muttered. "Orestes seems so sure. Yet it was such a small thing that I prayed for. Only that my master might not waken while I was writing the letter! It would have meant life to my mother!"

There was still a shred of hope that the peddler had been able to speak to his mother, or at least to give her the bit of woolen cloth. "If he failed—" Madoc's voice broke. He saw his mother wasting away at her loom because she had given up hope.

His lips grew tight. He must not think of that. Soon he would know. Winter was past, and the peddler would be returning.

When he reached home a man was standing at the door of the villa. Hannibal came in answer to his knock and took the letter that he handed in. Madoc slipped inside before the door was closed.

Cornelius came to the library doorway. The letter was given into his hands, and Madoc watched as he broke the seal. He listened as his master read in low tones: "Petronia, to Cornelius, my dearly loved husband. Peace be with you."

Madoc saw his master's face light up with happiness as he read on: "I have at last received permission from the emperor to come to you in Judea."

There was a whispered, "Thanks be to God!" then the reading went on: "Our little daughter is well. She longs for her father, even as I for my husband. Though the season be early for ocean travel, we take ship in seven days. At your command, I bring with me the slave—"

Suddenly Cornelius glanced up. He caught Madoc's steady gaze. "Well, well," he snapped, "must you stand and listen?"

Madoc backed from the room. He hurried to the stable to tell Hannibal the news. Petronia, the wife of Cornelius, had left Italy to come to Caesarea. She had left only a week later than the ship that had arrived today. That would mean, Madoc told Hannibal, that if all went well she should be in Caesarea in about seven days. She was bringing their little girl and at least one servant, for the letter had mentioned a slave.

Hannibal's white teeth gleamed in a broad smile. He left off brushing the satiny coat of the centurion's favorite horse. "Now that is good news, lad! Master has been praying for them to come. I have listened, when he didn't know Hannibal was near. He prays to this new God more and more."

Madoc ran his fingers through the horse's long mane. "And you, Hannibal, do you pray to the new God?"

Hannibal shook his head. He was still grinning cheerfully. "Master takes care of Hannibal."

Madoc persisted. "But if you knew that someone had said, 'Come unto me all ye that labor,' wouldn't you think that person cared what happened to you? Wouldn't he help you to do what you wanted?"

Hannibal flashed a puzzled glance at Madoc, then went on with his task. "Maybe soon a little child is coming. Hannibal can show her where the sparrows nest in the brush! Take her to the market place, maybe carry her on his shoulder!"

The African was going on and on. His dark face glistened with perspiration and delight.

Madoc interrupted. "Stop, Hannibal, and listen to me!"

Madoc was still thinking about his letter. "If there was something you wanted to do, something you had worked for and dreamed of doing for months and months—"

Hannibal turned with a jerk. "Now what you dreaming about? Want to run away again? Master told Hannibal to watch—"

Madoc stared as the African stopped in confusion. So the master had feared that he would try to escape. And Hannibal, he knew, would keep close watch now that ocean travel was again bringing ships into port after the winter storms.

He glared at Hannibal's sagging jaw. The African had obviously been told to keep silent but the words had slipped out. Madoc turned without a word and walked away.

CHAPTER 16: DAYS OF WAITING

When he left Hannibal, Madoc hurried back to the courtyard. There he could hear if Cornelius should summon him. He had not long to wait.

"Go to the market place," said his master. "Buy bread of the worth of this money and give it to the beggars who sit outside the city gates."

Madoc was surprised. He and Hannibal had already taken the usual alms to the poor of the town. He waited while Cornelius murmured with bowed head, "I would give thanks to the God who has heard my prayers—in the name of Jesus."

The centurion glanced up at Madoc, then down at the letter, still in his hands. A half smile pulled at his lips. "If I could only be sure," he muttered, "that Gratus has not made a mistake." Then he frowned and shook his head. "But no, I cannot be certain."

Madoc backed away. He had not understood all the words of his master, but he knew that the special alms were given as a thank offering because Cornelius' family was coming to him.

So his master's prayers were to be answered. His own, so small in comparison, had not been heard. There was only one answer, let Orestes say what he would. The truth was that the longing of a slave boy to free his mother was a matter of no importance to God.

In the week that followed, it was easy to see that Cornelius was happy. A faraway smile played across his lips and the ready frown came less often. Sometimes Madoc felt his master's gaze fixed on him. It was not an unfriendly look, but Madoc grew restless because he could not guess the reason for it.

There was great activity about the villa. Madoc spent many hours sweeping and sponging the tiled floors until they glowed with new beauty. The pool in the reception hall was emptied and scrubbed and filled with fresh water. The courtyard and garden were cleared of weeds. Rare fish were placed in the pool of the marble cherub. They were chosen to delight a little girl with their bright colors.

Madoc was given a tunic of soft gray wool and a girdle of red. Hannibal strutted about in a mantle of red and yellow strips, such as the dark-skinned Arabs wore.

By the end of the week Hannibal and Reuben had laid in a huge supply of sticks and roots for the oven. Anna, her black hair damp with perspiration, roasted chicken, baked bread and honey cakes. It was impossible to tell what day the ship would arrive, but Cornelius wanted to make certain that when it came, the feast would be prepared. As a result, much choice food was given to the poor to keep it from spoiling.

On the first day that the ship could be expected to arrive, Madoc found Orestes sitting on a mat outside his door. He was moving his arms and legs cautiously, as if the pain were easing a little in the sunshine of early spring.

"Peace be with you," Madoc said. "My master has sent you a roasted chicken and cakes sweetened with dates and honey. He prays that your health may be soon restored."

"Your master is kind," Orestes answered. "May the rich blessings of God be upon him and all his household."

Madoc said nothing. He put the food inside, then came back to sit beside his teacher. He took from the front of his tunic a worn parchment and prepared, as usual, to read.

Orestes held up his hand. "Wait." He studied the boy's questioning face. "It has been many days since I gave you the words of Jesus. Have you, perhaps, forgotten them?"

Madoc shook his head. He had tried to forget, but found that he could not. He repeated in a low voice, "'Come unto me all ye that labor and are heavy laden.'"

"Have they brought you any comfort, my son?"

Madoc's voice was bitter. "No, my lord! What meaning can they have to a slave boy who may have no god but his master?"

Orestes' voice was gentle. "Remember, I too have been a slave. You are heavy laden, lad?"

"Not with hard work or hunger," Madoc admitted, "and not with the floggings that are given to most slaves. But I asked so little! Only one small thing!"

He hesitated. What good would it do to tell Orestes? Then somehow the words burst out. "I asked of God only that I might send a letter to my mother. She is a slave in Italy. I prayed that my master might not waken while I was writing it."

He choked, then hurried on, his voice husky with bitterness. "But he did waken, and he took the letter from me. Now his prayer is being answered, for his family is coming across the sea. Perhaps even now the ship is coming into port."

Orestes' eyes were closed. Madoc was thankful, for he did not want the old man to see his twisting lips and trembling chin.

"It seemed good," Madoc hurried on, "when first I heard of the new Way. I decided to make trial of it. But now, something has gone from me."

The old man nodded in sympathy. "I know, lad, how hard you worked to prepare that letter. That must have been a sorry wound, when it was taken from you. But you must not forget that God has a plan for your life. A plan that will not always be clear to you." He smiled a little as he added, "Were you, perhaps, telling God what to do?"

Madoc's eyes opened wide. A slow flush mounted to his forehead. Was that what he had done when he prayed that his master might not waken while he was writing the letter? Was it?

The wind in a sudden gust whipped the hair from his forehead and blew it across his eyes. "My lord," he said, "I must have time to think about your words. Let me help you into the house. I fear a storm is blowing up."

Dark clouds were rolling in over the sea as Madoc started homeward without having read his lesson.

"O God," he whispered in to the wind, "hear now the prayer of your servant Madoc. I will try again to follow the Way."

He glanced seaward, at the gathering clouds. The wind caught at his cloak and pressed it against his body. Madoc drew a deep breath, then hurried on with a feeling that something hard and cold had melted in his chest.

When he entered the house, Cornelius was pacing back and forth. He called to Madoc.

"Go to the harbor and look out to sea. Watch for a ship bearing at her bows a figurehead of the twin gods, Castor and Pollux. If it comes, bring me word at once. If not, at the going down of the sun, come to me here."

Madoc drew his cloak back over his shoulders and raced down the hill. He hurried through the market place, where a few men and women sat huddled in their cloaks, heads bowed before the wind. Then he went on through the gates, past the shops and soldiers' barracks, to the wharf.

He walked to the end of the wharf and looked out. Two great stone arms extended far into the sea. They helped make a safe harbor for the ships that came with dyed stuffs from Tyre and Sidon, for fishing boats, and for the great sailing vessels of the Roman Empire.

There were no large ships tied to the wharf. Only a few small fishing boats were there, and a flat-bottomed lumber carrier loaded with cedar timbers from Lebanon. He looked up. The whole sky was dark and heavy with clouds.

Madoc lingered on the wharf until a dull red glow showed along the rim of the sea and he knew that the sun was near to setting. Then he hurried to get through the city gates before they should be closed for the night.

He entered the house through the courtyard. The heavy draperies that covered the doorways billowed inward with the push of the wind. He found Cornelius in the library.

"My lord, there was nothing."

Cornelius did not lift his head. Madoc waited, then went away quietly. In the kitchen he found Anna and Rueben and Hannibal, all moving about restlessly.

Anna looked up. "The master has not called for his supper. It has been ready and waiting for a long time. I know not what to do."

The kitchen was filled with tempting odors. Hannibal swallowed hungrily. "Um, if he could just smell that duck and fish—"

Madoc interrupted. "If we carry it through the library to the small dining room, perhaps he will look up and be reminded."

Madoc went first with a plate of shellfish smothered in an oily, peppery sauce. He walked slowly, watching his master's bent head. Hannibal followed with the roasted duck on a silver tray. They placed the food on the low table. Then Hannibal tiptoed back through the library to the kitchen.

"My lord," Madoc ventured, "your supper is waiting."

Cornelius got up without a word. He went to the dining room and lay down on a couch beside the table. As he reached for a shellfish, a sudden gust of wind caught at the flame of the saucer lamp on its high pedestal, making it flicker and almost go out.

Cornelius leaped to his feet. "I must do something!" he muttered. He began to pace back and forth at a furious rate. "I cannot lie here at my ease, eating and drinking!"

He glanced at the food, then up at Madoc. "Take it away!" he commanded.

Late in the night the wind died down. Madoc listened until the restless creakings of his master's bed grew still; then he, too, was able to sleep. In the morning he was roused at break of dawn and went again to the harbor to watch. A thick chilling fog lay over the water. He could see out only a few yards over the restless waves.

A small ship from Sidon ventured into port. Madoc watched as the bales of purple-red cloth were tossed from its deck, then carried away on the backs of slaves. He walked out again to the end of the wharf, but the fog shut out everything. Everything except the sound of the waves as they swelled against the rocks, then sank back.

At noon Hannibal came. Madoc watched as that long, swaying stride carried the African smoothly along the stone wharf.

"Master says for you to come home," he told Madoc. He stood leaning forward, trying to see through the milky fog. He shook his head. "Everybody praying for that ship to come in."

Madoc swept the misty drops from his lashes with the back of his hand. "And you, Hannibal—have you prayed, too?"

xMadoc hurried home. It was as Hannibal had said. Anna, in the kitchen, stirred the cooking pot while Reuben repeated over and over in his own tongue, "Have mercy upon us, O Lord, have mercy upon this house!"

Madoc found the centurion leaning against a pillar of the garden porch, his head bowed. Madoc waited. In the fog-laden room he could hear the bare branches of a fig tree scratching like skinny fingers against the rough stone of the garden wall.

Madoc sighed deeply. His master turned, a question in his eyes.

"I was not able to see anything, my lord, because of the fog. A ship might be outside the harbor, waiting for the fog to lift."

Madoc had hoped that his words might give a little cheer, but they sounded hollow in his own ears.

The centurion seemed not to have heard. He said, "Bring me bread and cheese in the library. Then prepare to go to the homes of the needy. They must not be forgotten in this unusual cold."

Later, Madoc went back to the harbor. Hannibal was there, walking up and down, trying to keep warm.

"Everything cold," he complained. "Cold outside, cold in

here." He placed a broad palm over his stomach. "Cold inside because that ship doesn't come."

And so passed that day, then another, and another. Madoc had lost count when, early one morning a breeze sprang up. He lay in his bed and listened to its sighing. Then a ray of sunshine broke through the narrow window high above his master's bed.

"Get up," called Cornelius, and there was new life in his voice. "Take your breakfast in your hand and run to the harbor. At sight of a ship, come back with all speed."

Madoc raced from the house. The city gates were just opening, and he hurried through the quiet streets to the wharf. There was no one else about, no sign of a sail moving across the water. After an hour he saw Cornelius coming toward him, his cloak held close about him.

The centurion's face was gray, and the frown was deep between his eyes. He said nothing as he came to stand beside Madoc. He placed a hand on the boy's shoulder. Madoc longed to remind his master that the ship was only a few days late. Instead, he remarked, "My lord, the tide has just turned. See, it is coming in."

There was no answer. Madoc stood very still, for he felt that somehow his master was leaning on him. Sea birds came and settled along the edge of the stone wharf. They lifted their white wings as they marched back and forth over the wet stones. Cornelius moved away to pace up and down beside them. His eyes were downcast. Madoc stared out to sea. Suddenly he leaned forward, his eyes growing narrower.

"Master!" he screamed. "Look there, toward the south! A ship!"

Cornelius turned. He came back to stand again beside Madoc. In a moment he cried out brokenly, "It is—oh, please God that it may be the ship I long to see!"

Together they waited, the man and the boy, no longer master and slave. The hand on his shoulder tightened until it hurt, but Madoc found relief in it from the tightening in his own throat.

Slowly, slowly the ship drew closer. Madoc could see that the sail was down, the mainmast smashed. But the oars were moving. With the eye of memory Madoc saw the galley slaves in the hold, sweating and gasping, straining to bring the ship into port.

Suddenly the grip on his shoulder loosened. The centurion flung both hands high above his head. "It is! It is! Oh, see there—at the prow, the figurehead of Castor and Pollux! To the living God be thanksgiving and praise!"

CHAPTER 17: A SHIP COMES IN

Madoc laughed unsteadily. Cornelius, without taking his eyes from the ship, shouted, "Go back to the villa! Tell Anna and Reuben to make ready the feast!"

Madoc waited on tiptoe, as if about to take wing. "Shall I return to you here?"

"No!"

The slave boy's high spirits came down with a jolt. All through the winter he had held to the hope that the Syrian peddler would have given the cloth to his mother. Though he might not have been able to speak to her, the cloth and a meaningful glance would tell her that her son lived and there was hope. And the peddler might be returning now, on the ship that was coming into port! Madoc longed to wait and see.

Cornelius was fumbling with his moneybag. "Go to the shops. Buy sweets and toys, such as a little girl would enjoy! Here is money. Now go!"

Madoc took the coins and ran. He thought Hannibal would never answer his banging on the knocker. Then, at his ringing shouts, the quiet villa sprang suddenly to life.

Racing back to town, Madoc went to the street of bakers,

then to the makers of toys and the sellers of dried fruits. It took a long time, for how was he to know what a little girl would like? He pictured the ship swinging about beside the wharf, then the meeting of Cornelius and his family. Perhaps even now they were back at the villa.

As he started homeward, he passed the tavern. He glanced inside. His heart leaped, then pounded thickly. There in the room that was open to the street sat the Syrian peddler!

Madoc darted inside. His basket of sweets and toys dropped to the floor. "Oh, sir," he cried out, "you have returned!"

The man set down his cup and looked around. He stared, as if he did not know the boy who faced him. "Go away," he growled. "What have I to do with you?"

"Sir, don't you remember? You were to find my mother! You promised to give her a piece of cloth and perhaps a message."

"I promised nothing!" shouted the peddler.

"But you promised to try and, don't you remember, I gave you five denarii?"

The man's mouth drew down in an ugly sneer. "And now, because I was not able to speak to her, I suppose you expect me to give back the money? Go away! You are wasting your time."

"You did give her the bit of cloth, didn't you?"

"No!" Then the peddler added in a sulky growl, "She was not there."

Madoc turned sick with fear. "What did you learn of her? She—oh, she is not dead?"

"How should I know?" The Syrian picked up his cup and drank deeply, then wiped his mouth on the back of his hand before he added, "The weaver told me only that she had been sold. Her new owner was taking her to a foreign land."

Madoc drew a long, tired breath. His body swayed and he caught at the edge of the table to keep from falling. "If she could only have had the cloth!" he mumbled brokenly. "It would have helped her, just to know that I am alive. That I—tried to keep the vow!"

His voice broke in a dry, shuddering sob.

The peddler laughed unpleasantly. "Eh, that precious cloth!" He reached into his knapsack. "I had forgotten to throw it away. Here it is. Take it, and leave me in peace!" He flung the bit of checkered wool to the floor.

Madoc picked it up, stumbled out of the tavern, and walked away. So it had not mattered after all that he had not been able to send the letter. Now nothing mattered. Not even the freedom for which he had planned through every hour of his slavery. That hope, which had been like the ground beneath his feet, had dropped away. Nothing solid was left.

Madoc was nearly at the city gates before he remembered his basket. He went back and picked up the toys and sweetmeats, then stumbled toward home. Slipping around the garden wall, he entered through the barnyard gate. He placed the basket on the floor, just inside the kitchen door. He was about to slip away, but Anna met him in the courtyard.

"So you are back at last! Hannibal has been searching for you all over the town. He had a wild idea that you might have run away. You are to go to the master at once!"

Madoc said nothing. His feet dragged. Anna leaned from the kitchen doorway. She called sharply, "At once! Do you hear?"

Across the courtyard and into the great front room Madoc walked, dull-eyed. He glanced up briefly, then stopped. Cornelius was there, seated on a couch beside his wife. In his arms he held a little dark-haired girl.

Madoc waited, his arms folded across his chest.

Cornelius saw him and spoke. "Petronia, this is the young slave of whom I wrote. Madoc, come here."

Madoc shuffled closer.

"My son!" The Roman's voice was gentle, and in the pause that followed, Madoc wondered why his master should speak so to him, a slave. Then, as the silence grew long, Madoc looked up.

"My son," Cornelius said again, "I am sorry to have made you unhappy about the letter to your mother. But I feared to tell you of my plans because it would have caused you even more grief if Gratus had failed, or if he had made a mistake."

Madoc still stood in puzzled silence. His master's words made no sense at all. The proud Roman seemed actually sorry for a slave's unhappiness. But how was Gratus concerned with that?

Madoc lifted his eyes in silent question. Was he expected to say or do something? Cornelius said in answer, "Go into the garden, Madoc."

For his lessons? Was it possible that Orestes had been able to come to the villa? Was his teacher waiting for him in the garden?

Madoc backed out through the archway to the porch. There he turned and looked about for Orestes. Instead, he saw a woman sitting on the marble bench. Her face was turned from him, but he could see that her head was thrown back, drinking in the clear spring sunshine. He could tell that her body drooped and the arm that lay across her lap was white and thin. But her hair—her hair was as yellow as his own!

He stared. His throat grew tight, then his breath came out in a noisy gasp.

The woman started and opened her eyes. She turned. Then she held out her hands. "Madoc! My son!"

"Mother!" All at once he was there in her arms, knowing nothing, hearing nothing but the joy that sang in his heart.

When both grew quiet, Greta wiped away his tears, then her own.

"Gratus came to the weaving mill and bought me," she explained. "He took me to a beautiful villa in the country. There the gracious lady Petronia read your letter to me. I was faint with joy."

Remembering, she could not go on. And now the strange words of his master were made clear to Madoc. "If Gratus had failed or made a mistake." A mistake, in buying the wrong slave!

Good, good Gratus! He had made no mistake. Madoc forgave him now all his small sins of the past. They were blotted out, as if they had never been.

Cornelius had planned it! This joy beyond all imagining!

He caught up the hand that rested in his own. "Come, Mother, with me."

Together they went into the house. Cornelius was standing, his hands behind his back, as if he were making a speech. He was facing the door that led into the courtyard. He turned as the two came from the garden to stand before him.

Madoc folded his hands across his chest, but he did not kneel. "Good master," he said, "let me serve you with all the strength of my body, for all the years of my life!"

Cornelius caught his shoulder and shook him affectionately. "Not so, my son! In the letter to your mother you wrote that someday you planned to be free."

Madoc's face grew hot, his tongue awkward. "B-but, my lord, my plans are not now what they were! Oh, please believe me, I am indeed sorry!"

Cornelius grinned cheerfully. "For what, my son? Have I not told you that your learning would be wasted in the camp of a soldier? And now that I am a follower of the Way, I am finding it hard to carry out the orders that come to me. I would have more time to study and to do the works of the Master. And so"—he smiled every more broadly—"as soon as my term here is ended, we shall all return to my farm in Italy."

He glanced toward the courtyard doorway. "All, that is, except Reuben and Anna. They shall be free to stay in their homeland."

Now Madoc noticed a strange purring sound. It came from the direction that Cornelius' glance had taken. Madoc looked up. There stood Hannibal, his dark face almost hidden behind a dazzling smile. He was singing his delight in a husky rumbling that came from deep in his throat.

Reuben was there, too, looking more confused than ever before. He held tightly to Anna's wrist while she wept happily against his shoulder.

Cornelius waved them away. Then he spoke again—this time, only to Madoc. "I may not free you now, lad, for the law of Rome forbids it. But you shall be like a son to me. And when you are a man, you will be free to return to your homeland. You, and your mother, too. There, if that is God's plan for you, perhaps you may lead others to become followers of the good new Way."

Madoc's mouth dropped open. He wanted to shout aloud his thanksgiving, but the words would not come.

Cornelius shook him with pretended roughness. "Ho, lad, have you lost the use of your tongue? Take your mother and go. Do not show your faces again until hunger calls you home."

Suddenly Madoc's white teeth gleamed in a smile that was almost as wide as Hannibal's. "Your word, good master, is my law."

He backed away, holding fast to his mother's hand. At the door they turned to walk through the courtyard. The sun was shining. Sparrows twittered in the hedge. Bees were humming about the blossoming mulberry tree.

Madoc stopped beside the tiled pool. "Mother," he said, "I used to believe that all the world belonged to Rome. Now I know that is not true. Today—thanks to God and our good master—today it belongs to us."